William Harper Littlejohn, the bespectacled scientist who was the world's greatest living expert on geology and archaeology.

Colonel John Renwick, "Renny," his favorite sport was pounding his massive fists through heavy, paneled doors.

Lieutenant Colonel Andrew Blodgett Mayfair, "Monk," only a few inches over five feet tall, and yet over 260 pounds. His brutish exterior concealed the mind of a great scientist.

Major Thomas J. Roberts, "Long Tom," was the physical weakling of the crowd, but a genius at electricity.

Brigadier General Theodore Marley Brooks, slender and waspy, he was never without his ominous, black, sword-cane.

TOGETHER WITH THEIR LEADER, THEY WOULD GO ANYWHERE, FIGHT ANYONE, DARE EVERYTHING—SEEKING EXCITEMENT AND PERILOUS ADVENTURE!

Books by Kenneth Robeson

🐦 Published by Bantam Books

THE MYSTIC MULLAH

A Doc Savage Adventure

By Kenneth Robeson

THE MYSTIC MULLAH

*A Bantam Book / published by arrangement with
The Condé Nast Publications Inc.*

PRINTING HISTORY

Originally published in DOC SAVAGE *Magazine January 1935
Bantam edition published November 1965*

*Bantam Books are published by Bantam Books, Inc., a subsidiary
of Grosset & Dunlap, Inc. Its trade-mark, consisting of the words
"Bantam Books" and the portrayal of a bantam, is registered in the
United States Patent Office and in other countries. Marca Registrada.
Bantam Books, Inc., 271 Madison Avenue, New York, N. Y. 10016.*

PRINTED IN THE UNITED STATES OF AMERICA

THE MYSTIC MULLAH

Chapter 1

THE BROKEN NECK

It was a drizzling gray evening full of moaning ghosts. The rain came down in occasional flurries, but most of the time it remained suspended in the air as mist that the newspapers next day were to call "the thickest fog within memory." Harbor traffic was almost at a standstill, and only those boat captains who were foolhardy, or those pressed by absolute necessity, were abroad. The foghorns of the boats were the moaning ghosts.

One ghost was especially persistent. It had the particular strident voice peculiar to tugboat whistles, and it came up through the Narrows from the open sea at a clip that put cold chills on the spines of boatmen who knew how thick that fog was.

There was something scared, something imperative, and maybe something a bit mad about the tooting of that tugboat. A coast guard cutter became interested and nosed over to investigate. Coast guardsmen will go out in anything.

The cutter skipper nosed in close, saw that the tug was the *Whale of Gotham*, and that there was a picture of a spouting whale painted on the bows. Then, after the manner of coast guard skippers with tugboat captains, the cutter commandant swore a blue streak.

"What's the idea of tearing in here like an express train?" he finished.

The tugboat master swore back. He would have been very polite to another tugboat captain, but a coast guard skipper was fair game.

"Sheer off!" he yelled. "I've got a man aboard, who's been hurt! We're rushing him to a hospital. He's dying!"

It was a story that satisfied even the coast guardsman, so he sheered off and betook himself away in the fog. And that set the tugboat captain to chuckling.

A voice at the tugboat captain's elbow spoke an English that was entirely too perfect.

"Why did you tell him that?" it asked. "We have no dying man aboard."

1

The tug master jumped as if a transatlantic liner had shoved out of the fog at full speed. He turned, an angry exclamation on his tongue, for he did not like to be startled, especially in this fog, with his nerves already on edge. But he held his counsel, for the man at his elbow did not look like one who would take a tongue-lashing; and furthermore, it would be bad policy to insult a man who is paying a tremendous sum for the services of your tugboat.

The man had a big hooked nose and a beard that was small and pointed. His skin was a yellow-brown, dry and wrinkled, and did not appeal to the eye. He wore strange garments.

The tugboat skipper had done his life's traveling in New York harbor, so he did not know that the long, flowing white mantle which reached down from the hook-nosed man's head was an *abah*, or that his embroidered cloak was a *jubbah*, or that the queer-looking trousers were *shirwals*. Only one who had traveled in Central Asia would know what the garments were called.

On the hook-nosed man's forehead was a strange design, an affair of lines which might have been construed as a likeness of a serpent coiled around a jewel, as if protecting it. The lines looked as if they were put on with ink, but actually they were tattooed into the skin with a fluid that one of the master sorcerers of Asia had insisted was composed partially of the dried blood of Genghis Khan, the original.

To the tugboat captain, the mark looked like a dirty smear; and had he known its true significance, he might have fallen off the bridge of his grimy craft. For it was the Sacred Seal of the Khan Nadir Shar, Son of Divinity, Destined Master of Ten Thousand Lances, Khan of Tanan, Ruler of Outer Mongolia. Maybe the tug skipper would not have known what all of that meant. Probably not.

It meant that the hook-nosed man, Khan Shar, was a king, absolute ruler of the city of Tanan, beyond Outer Mongolia, and monarch over the surrounding provinces.

"Advise me when we tie up at the dock," requested Khan Shar in his too-perfect English.

"Sure," said the skipper.

"This dock you have selected—it is secluded?" asked the Khan.

The skipper rolled his tobacco quid in his jaws. The man made him nervous.

"It's an out-of-the-way dock," he said.

"Excellent!" said the Khan, and left the tugboat bridge, or more properly, the pilot house.

The tugboat captain rolled his eyes and directed tobacco juice at the feet of one of his two deckhands, who had come in out of the foggy night.

"Damned if I like this," he said in a tone which showed he wanted to talk to relieve his mind.

The deckhand, who knew that tone, let his boss talk without interruption.

"Damned if I like it," repeated the skipper. "I get a radio to go out to the *Atlantic Queen,* that new liner that's fog bound, and take off a passenger. I get out there, and, by golly, if it ain't three passengers, and two of 'em the queerest-lookin' ducks you ever saw! Take that one who was just in here."

"I'd rather take him than the other man," said the deckhand in a queer tone.

The skipper scowled. "Whatcha mean?"

"I mean that the other duck has a knife as long as your arm up his sleeve," said the deckhand. "I just saw it. He's standin' outside the door of your cabin. Looks like he's guardin' the girl."

"The girl!" The skipper sighed. "Now she's what I call a nifty number. She's white, too. Wonder what she's doin' with these two funny-lookin' buzzards?"

The skipper was not a bad judge of femininity. The girl *was* a "nifty number." In fact, she would have put a movie casting director up on his toes.

She was tall, with dark hair and lashes that were altogether delectable. But there was something else about her. She was businesslike, capable. Her person radiated efficiency.

Her clothing was thoroughly modern, and so was the blue automatic which she held in her hand as the door opened.

The hook-nosed Khan Shar looked at the gun and smiled as if it might have been a cocktail the young woman intended offering him.

"I do not feel there is danger," he said. "We have not heard of the Mystic Mullah since our caravan left the Gobi."

The girl kept the gun in her hands. "A thousand lives depend on what we are doing," she said dryly. "If you want to be dramatic, you can put the figure higher."

The Khan's dark face drained of its color, giving him a stark, agonized look.

"You could put the figure higher—and not be dramatic," he said thickly.

Neither spoke again, for the tugboat engine had changed its regular pulse and was running slowly; it accelerated, then pounded, as if the craft were backing. Shouts rang out, and scraping sounds on deck indicated ropes dragging. There was a bump, rather violent, then lesser bumps and the tug heeled so that the Khan put out a hand to steady himself. There were four large rings, each with a big jewel, on his fingers.

"I trust we have tied to a secluded dock," said the Khan.

"Hadim!" called the girl.

The door opened and a lean man with a long, brown face came in. He was dressed in a flowing *jubbah* and *shirwals* that fitted his legs tightly, and he carried his left arm stiffly, as if not wishing to disturb the long knife which the deckhand had seen up that sleeve.

This Hadim did not present an appealing picture, for some one had made a pass at him with a sword or a knife in the past, and had come just close enough to groove his face with a permanent scar from forehead to chin. He bowed deeply to the girl.

"Yes, Miss Joan," he said.

"You will leave at once, Hadim," said the girl. "You know what you are to do, the message you are to deliver. And you know how much depends upon our finding this man."

"Yes, Miss Joan," said Hadim. "My four brothers, my father and mother and my sisters have died when touched by the green soul of the Mystic Mullah. Need I more to remind me?"

"You will die if you make a mistake," said the girl. "And if we do not reach this man we have come to see, many more may follow you. Just how many, there is no telling." She extended her automatic. "Better take this."

Hadim tapped his sleeve. "I know better how to use this."

Joan directed, "Have the man get in touch with us."

Hadim murmured, "Aye, and this man's name is——"

"Doc Savage," said Joan. "Hurry. We must find him, or learn where he is."

There was rawness in the fog, a damp chill, and the vapor had long since washed the moon and stars out of the sky and had put the dank water-front streets in the grip of the clammy mist from the sea.

Hadim embraced the soupy fog as one at home in his element, and he took to the shabby, narrow water-front thoroughfares without hesitation. He did, however, walk in the middle of the street—until almost run down by a prowling taxicab. Hadim looked the hack over carefully, after the driver stopped to see if he had done any damage. The driver had an honest face, so Hadim used his cab to go uptown.

Hadim, let out at his destination, stared up at the building which he was to enter, and stark amazement sat upon his scarred, brown face. This building was the pride of native New Yorkers. To Hadim, it was an architectural wonder such as he had not dreamed existed. It was a modernistic structure, somewhere near a hundred stories in height, and was a blinding exhibition of white stone and shining metal.

"What a lot of camels would be needed to haul the stones for this house," Hadim murmured.

Then he went inside, asked questions, made a few mistakes, but eventually got in an elevator which let him out, after a frightsome ride upward, on the eighty-sixth floor. The corridor was as impressive as the building exterior.

"Even the palace of the Khan does not excel this," Hadim told himself.

Then he jerked to a stop. He could feel a slight breeze through the corridor. And he had heard a hissing sound. This last was very faint.

Hadim turned slowly—and his voice went out in a sudden, wild shriek of terror. It was ear-splitting, that shriek. In it was all of the agony of a man who knows he has met death.

Down the corridor, floating in the air, strange, fantastic things were approaching. They were like fat snakes, their color an unholy green, their diameter perhaps that of a human wrist, their length the span of an arm from hand to elbow. They whirled, contorted with a sort of dervish dance. They seemed to grow fatter, then thinner.

Most hideous of all was the fact that these flying serpentine things seemed unreal. They were ghostly, nebulous, without any real body or shape.

Hadim, screaming again, had his long knife out of his left sleeve. He retreated. The green things overhauled him. He began to run backward. They still gained.

Hadim came to the end of the corridor, to a window. He beat it, knocking the glass out, but the metal crosspieces defied him, thwarting him in his mad desire to jump through.

The green horrors reached him and Hadim struck with his knife, only to shriek out in fresh horror as the blade passed completely through the green atrocity and nothing happened. He struck again; then the serpentine things were upon him.

They brushed against his arms, his chest. One rolled like a hideous green tongue, caressing his face, lingering about his mouth, his nostrils, then rolling up over his eyes. Hadim fought them with his hands, shrieking again and again; he writhed down to get away from them, and squirmed on the floor.

Then the green things arose and drifted out through the holes which Hadim had beaten in the skyscraper window with his fists. They went slowly, as if satisfied with the work they had done. They had changed shape materially by now; one had been knocked to pieces and had resolved itself into half a dozen thin, green strings, so pale that the eye could easily see through them, distinguishing the frames of the window behind them.

Chapter 2

THE FIRE-FACED MAN

Down the corridor a way, and around a corner, there was a plain metal door, the panel of which bore a name in small letters of a peculiar bronze color:

CLARK SAVAGE, JR.

This door whipped back and a tall, incredibly bony man popped out. The man was thinner than it seemed any human being could be and still exist. He wore no coat, and a rubber apron was tied about his midsection. Rubber gloves were on his hands, and one hand held a magnifying glass made in the shape of a monocle.

He peered about, blinking, searching for the source of the shrieks which had drawn his attention. But there was a crook in the corridor and he did not see the form of Hadim immediately.

The bony man absently stowed the monocle magnifier in a vest pocket under his rubber laboratory apron, and advanced. He rounded the corner, jerked up and stared.

Hadim was now motionless on the floor, and his head was angled back in a grotesque posture which no man could attain normally.

The bony man in the rubber apron suddenly snapped a hand to an armpit and brought it away gripping a weapon which somewhat resembled an oversize automatic pistol. He flipped this up and tightened on the trigger; the weapon shuttled, smoked and made a noise like a gigantic bullfiddle. It was a machine pistol with a tremendous firing speed.

One of the sinister green wraiths was still inside the corridor, rolling against the window as if seeking blindly to escape. The stream of bullets from the machine pistol passed through it, disturbing it, fattening it a little, but not destroying it or seeming in any way to affect its unholy life.

The stream of lead broke glass out of the window. The green harpy squirmed through the opening and floated away

7

into the gloom, losing itself over the nest of skyscraper spires.

The skeleton of a man stood very still for a long minute. "I'll be superamalgamated!" he muttered finally.

Stooping, he examined the body of Hadim—body, for Hadim was dead. When Hadim's head was moved, there was a grisly looseness about its attachment to the body, as if it were only connected by a cord no stiffer than a wrapping twine.

The bony man eyed Hadim's extraordinarily long knife.

"Sixteenth century Tananese," he decided aloud. Then he employed the monocle magnifier briefly. "Wrong. Tananese, all right, but of modern construction, using sixteenth century methods of tempering and moulding. Most peculiar."

The wall beside Hadim's body was of plaster, painted over, and it was scarred with numerous rather odd-looking marks. These came to the thin man's attention.

"I'll be superamalgamated!" he gulped again, using what was evidently, for him, a pet ejaculation. He stared harder at the marks. Down the corridor, an elevator door clanked to a stop. Before the door opened, voices could be heard. They were very loud voices, angry. It sounded as if a fight was about to occur in the elevator. The cage door opened and a man came skidding out.

This man was slender, waspish, with a high forehead and a large orator's mouth. His attire was sartorial perfection from silken topper to the exact hang of his tail coat. He carried a thin, black cane.

He yelled at the open elevator door, "You hairy accident! You awful mistake of nature! You insult to the human race!"

A most striking-looking individual now came out of the elevator. His height was no greater than that of a young boy; his width was almost equal to his height. His face was mostly mouth, with a broken nubbin of a nose, small eyes set in pits of gristle, and scarcely a noticeable quantity of forehead. His long arms dangled well below his knees and the wrists were matted with hair that looked like rusted steel wool.

Had the corridor been a little less brilliantly lighted, the hairy gentleman might have been mistaken for an amiable gorilla.

The hairy man squinted little eyes at the dapper one, and said, "Pipe down, you shyster, or I'll tie a knot in your neck!"

Then they both saw the tall skeleton of a man down the corridor. They could not help but note his excitement.

"What's happened, Johnny?" demanded the apish fellow. They could not see the body of Hadim, which lay around the bend in the corridor.

"Johnny," the bony man—he was actually William Harper Littlejohn, world-renowned expert on archæology and geology—gestured over his shoulder with the monocle magnifier.

"Come here, Monk," he said, then included the dapper man. "You too, Ham."

"Monk," the homely gorilla of a man, and "Ham," the immaculate fashion plate, advanced hurriedly. A moment before, they had seemed on the point of blows; now their quarrel was suddenly suspended. It was always thus. No one who knew these two could recall one having addressed a civil word to the other.

Monk, whose low forehead did not look as if it afforded room for more than a spoonful of brains, was Lieutenant Colonel Andrew Blodgett Mayfair, generally conceded to be one of the most accomplished of industrial chemists; while Ham, the fashion plate, was Major General Theodore Marley Brooks, a lawyer who possessed probably the sharpest legal mind ever trained by Harvard.

Monk and Ham, rounding the hallway angle and sighting Hadim's body with its grotesquely twisted head, jerked to a stop and became slack-jawed.

"Blazes!" Monk sniffed, sampling the air like an animal. "I smell burned gunpowder. Who shot the guy?"

"No one," said Johnny. "I fired a few shots subsequently."

Monk ambled over to the body, hands swinging below his knees, and stared intently.

"What's wrong with his neck?" he asked.

"Broken," Johnny replied.

Monk asked, "Who broke it?"

"No one," answered the gaunt geologist. "As far as I can tell."

"Yeah," Monk growled. "Then who'd you shoot at?"

"A peculiar, nebulous green corporeity with the optical aspects of a serpentine specimen suspended aërospherically," said Johnny, his expression not changing. "It bore similarity to a phantasmagoria."

Monk lifted one hand and snapped thumb and forefinger loudly.

"Now do it again with little words," he requested.

Johnny had once held the chair of natural science research in a famous university where he had been known as a professor who stunned most of his students with his big words, and he still had the habit. He never used a small word when he could think of a large one.

"A green thing was floating in the air above the body," said Johnny. "I shot. The bullet went through it, breaking the window. Then the thing floated out through the window and away."

Monk said unsmilingly, "I always did think those big words would drive you crazy."

Johnny pointed at the odd-looking marks scratched on the wall beside Hadim's body.

"The man obviously inscribed these when he felt demise imminent," he said. "He used the tip of his knife."

Monk bent over, looked and said, "They don't mean anything. He just dug the wall with his knife as he was flopping around."

"Those marks," said Johnny, "are words, or word signs, rather, of Tananese, an obscure language with an Arabic derivative, spoken in certain parts of outer Mongolia."

"What do they say?" asked Monk.

And Johnny, who probably knew as many ancient languages, written and spoken, as any half dozen of the ordinary so-called experts on the subject, drew a paper and pencil from his pocket and reproduced thereon the characters which the wall bore, here and there correcting a stroke which Hadim, in his dying agony, had made with slight error. Then Johnny wrote the English translation under the word signs. He passed it to Monk and Ham. They read:

MANY LIVES WILL BE SPARED IF HE OF MOUNTAINS WHO CHARMS EVIL SPIRITS WILL GO TO FISH THAT SMOKES ON WATER WHERE THE KHAN SHAR AND JOAN———

"It ends there," said Johnny. "You can see the name 'Joan' is scratched out in the nearest thing an Asiatic could come to English letters."

Ham, the dapper lawyer, fumbled absently with his slim black cane, and in doing so, separated the handle slightly from the rest of the cane, revealing that there was a long, slender blade of razor-sharp steel housed in the cane body.

"That sounds silly," he said. "What does it mean?"

Monk suddenly banged a fist on a knee, something he could do without stooping.

"Remember that radio we got a few days ago?" he demanded. "The message was signed, 'Joan Lyndell.'"

The gaunt Johnny said sharply, "I have been carrying it around with me," and withdrawing a radiogram blank from a pocket, he passed it to the others, open for perusal. They had all seen it before, but they went over it again:

DOC SAVAGE,
NEW YORK.
YOUR ASSISTANCE IMPERATIVE ON MATTER INVOLVING THOUSANDS OF LIVES AND POSSIBLY STABILITY OF WESTERN CIVILIZATION. PLEASE RADIO ME APPOINTMENT TIME AND PLACE. MY LINER WILL REACH NEW YORK THREE DAYS.
JOAN LYNDELL,
ABOARD S.S. ATLANTIC QUEEN.

Below the message, written in pencil, was another missive, one evidently penned as an answer to the radiogram. It read:

JOAN LYNDELL,
CARE TRANSATLANTIC LINER
ATLANTIC QUEEN.
SORRY BUT DOC SAVAGE NOT IN CITY AND NOT AVAILABLE TO COMMUNICATION. CANNOT SAY WHEN HE WILL RE-TURN.
WILLIAM HARPER LITTLEJOHN.

Monk rubbed his jaw and asked, "Connection?"

"Between this message and the dead man?" Johnny shrugged. "He inscribed the name 'Joan' on the wall."

Ham pointed at the wall markings with his sword cane. "But what does the rest of that mean?"

In the manner of a scholar giving a lecture, Johnny said, "The man could not write Doc Savage's name, so he came as near to describing it as he could. The mountain men in the Tananese region are savages, so 'He of Mountains' probably is meant for Savage. And a Tananese doctor is called one who chases evil spirits."

Monk squinted admiringly. "Maybe there *is* something besides big words in that head. What about the 'fish that smokes on water'?"

"A boat," said Johnny. "A boat in some manner connected with a fish, and probably an oil or a coal burner."

Ham said briskly, "I'll see about this."

He strode down the corridor, opened the door on which was the name "Clark Savage, Jr.," in small bronze letters, and entered a reception room which held an enormous safe, a costly inlaid table, and various other items of quiet but expensive furniture. Ham picked up a telephone.

With the casual ease of a man who had done the thing before, Ham got a land-line-radio connection to the liner *Atlantic Queen.* He spoke for some minutes, then hung up.

He did not leave the telephone immediately, but consulted the directory, then made a second call. Then he went out and joined the others.

"His Majesty, Khan Nadir Shar of Tanan, and a young woman named Joan Lyndell were taken off the *Atlantic Queen* by the tug *Whale of Gotham* about three hours ago," he repeated. "I called the owners of the *Whale of Gotham.* The tug is tied up at a wharf in the Hudson, off Twenty-sixth Street."

"*Whale of Gotham,*" Monk grunted. "That would be the 'fish that smokes on the water.'"

Ham eyed Johnny, then indicated the body of Hadim. "Just what did kill this fellow?"

The thin geologist shook his head slowly. "That is a profound mystery, as great a mystery as the nature of the green body I saw."

Monk frowned at Johnny, at the rubber apron the tall geologist wore. "Busy, aren't you?"

"Yes," Johnny admitted. "I am trying to assemble the vertebræ of a small dinosaur of the early Mesozoic——"

"Stick here," Monk advised. "Me and the tailor's dream here will go down to this tugboat."

"Very well," Johnny agreed, after hesitating.

"If Doc Savage shows up, tip him off," Monk finished.

Monk and Ham, departing, rode down to the basement in a private high-speed elevator which had undoubtedly cost a young fortune to install, and came out in a subterranean garage which held several motor vehicles, ranging from an open roadster of expensive manufacture and quiet color scheme to a large delivery van which, although it did not look the part, was literally an armored tank.

The elevator, the garage, the assortment of cars, as well as the establishment on the eighty-sixth floor—there was an enormous scientific laboratory and a highly complete scientific library up there in addition to the reception room—were all a part of the New York headquarters maintained by Doc Savage.

A strange individual, this Doc Savage. Probably one of the most remarkable of living men. A genius, a mental marvel and a giant of fabulous physical strength.

He was literally a product of science himself, was this Doc Savage, for he had been trained from birth for one single purpose in life—the fantastic career which he now followed. Every trick of science had been utilized in his training. In no sense had he led a life that might be regarded as normal.

Two hours of each day since childhood had been devoted to a routine of intense exercises calculated to develop not only muscles, but physical senses and mental sharpness. All of his early life had been devoted to study under masters of trades, sciences, professions, until he possessed a knowledge that was, to the ordinary man, uncanny.

The result of this studied upbringing was an individual who was a remarkable combination of scientific genius and physical capacity.

Stranger even than the man himself was the career to which his life was dedicated—the business of helping others out of trouble, of aiding the oppressed, of dealing with those evildoers who seemed beyond the touch of the law. For all of which Doc Savage made it an unbending rule to accept no payment in money, under any circumstances.

Long ago, Doc Savage had assembled five men as his assistants, five men who were world-famed specialists in their respective lines, five men who associated themselves with him because they loved adventure, excitement, and because they were drawn by admiration for the giant of bronze who was Doc Savage.

Monk, the chemist, and Ham, the lawyer, were two of the five aides. Johnny, the archæologist, was another. Two others —Colonel John "Renny" Renwick, engineer, and Major Thomas J. "Long Tom" Roberts, electrical wizard—were, at the moment, elsewhere in the city, engaged in the private business which they carried on when not actively assisting Doc Savage.

The present whereabouts of Doc Savage himself was something that no one knew. The bronze man had vanished. He had told no one where he was going. No one, not even his five aides, knew how to reach him. But they were not worried, these five, for they were confident that the bronze man had gone away to some mysterious rendezvous, where he could be alone for intensive study.

And, although Doc's five aides were not sure, they believed this place to which the bronze man retired, this remote trysting place with reflection which he called his Fortress of Solitude, was located on an island in the remote Arctic. It was certain, though, that no one would hear of Doc Savage until he should return, mysteriously as he had gone.

Monk and Ham, nearing the Hudson River water-front in a coupe which presented no outward hint that it was a rolling fortress with bullet-proof glass and armored body, exchanged comments punctuated with insults.

"We should've asked that walkin' encyclopedia, Johnny, more questions," Monk grumbled. "Where's Tanan, the place where this Khan Shar is supposed to be a king?"

"Didn't you study geography?" Ham asked sarcastically.

"Well, where is it?"

"In Asia."

Monk scowled. "Do you, or do you not, know where it is?"

"I know as much about it as you do," Ham snapped.

"Which is not a dang thing." Monk used a spotlight to ascertain a street number. "What's this king over here for? And what's he want with Doc?"

"Nothing was said about the king wanting Doc," Ham pointed out. "It was this Joan Lyndell who sent that radiogram."

Monk said, "Wonder who she is?"

"How would I know?" Ham said sourly.

They parked the car and got out. Monk rummaged for a flashlight, but was unable to find one, then they moved away from the machine.

Monk mused aloud, "Wonder what broke that brown-skinned guy's neck. Wish we'd figured that out."

Ham began, "Say, you hairy baboon—*wuh!*" He ended the statement with a sort of choked explosion.

Monk's jaw sagged, pulling his big mouth open cavernously; his fingers made absent straying movements. His little eyes seemed on the point of jumping from their pits of gristle.

They had been moving along a warehouse side, a wall of brick, unbroken by windows or other apertures. The darkness was intense.

Ahead of them, a face had appeared, materializing with an eerie unexpectedness. This was all the more startling, because the darkness was so thick that neither Monk nor Ham could see the other. Yet they saw the face clearly.

It was a fantastic thing, that face. Its color was not human, but a greenish hue, the tint that comes to meat in the first stages of decay. The green countenance shone with a fantastic luminosity; it was not exactly fluorescent, nor did it seem to have a light playing upon it, yet it was plainly visible.

The face had slant eyes, the contour of the Orient, and when it rolled lips back in a grin, the effect was anything but pleasant, for the tongue in the mouth, which should have been in shadow, was as plainly discernible as the other features. It was the same unholy green.

Monk said, "What the devil?" thickly.

Chapter 3

THE MYSTIC MULLAH TALKS

It was very silent beside the warehouse, for Monk and Ham were too surprised for further speech. Somewhere near, waves lapped with sounds like women sobbing, and farther away, there was a hissing, as of steam escaping from the boilers of a tugboat. Out in the harbor, whistles and foghorns still made occasional clamor in the thick fog.

The face hung suspended, like something disembodied, for the darkness was too thick to permit Monk and Ham to see the nature of the body to which it was attached. The effect was ghostly.

When the unearthly green lips writhed and words came from the verdant face, both Monk and Ham jumped. They could not help it.

"Try to control your surprise," the voice said.

Monk growled, "What the heck kind of hocus pocus is this, anyhow?"

"Do not jump at conclusions, my friends," said the voice. "You of the Western civilization are too prone to try to make science explain all that you see. You like to call all exhibitions of the occult by the plain terms of magic, meaning mechanical fakery. You make the mistake of not believing in the occult, the supernatural. Your minds are too practical."

"Jove!" Ham said vaguely. "I do not get this."

Monk grunted, "Why the lecture?"

The voice—it was hollow and unreal—went on.

"You are looking at something now that you do not understand," it said. "You think you see a face. Perhaps you think you see my body. You are wrong. You see neither face nor body."

"Nuts!" Monk felt under an arm where nestled a padded holster holding a machine pistol scarcely larger than an ordinary automatic.

"In a material sense," said the fantastic voice, "you are looking at a nonentity, at nothing. You think you see a face; but actually, there is nothing."

Monk got his machine pistol out, and directed sourly, "All

right, I guess half a pound or so of lead won't hurt you, Mr. Nonentity."

"Listen to me," said the voice. "I am the green soul of the Mystic Mullah. I am the master of all souls, the power infinite. I have touched many men, so that they have died and their souls come to me."

Ham unsheathed his sword cane. He preferred the weapon, because the tip was coated with a drug concoction which produced a quick, temporary unconsciousness.

The voice of the Mystic Mullah droned on, and there was no perceptible lip motion on the uncanny green face.

"Go back," it said. "Forget what has happened to-night. Forget it so thoroughly that you will not remember to tell this bronze man, Doc Savage."

Monk laughed; he laughed loudly, for somehow it made him feel better to hear the crash of his own false mirth.

Ham said dryly, "Very dramatic, Mr. Green Soul. Our lives are in danger, too, I suppose?"

"Only your physical bodies," said the voice. "Your souls will live on, green, serpentine, ghostly worms that travel in the night and do my bidding."

Monk thought of the green things which Johnny had seen. He began to perspire.

"I died a million years ago, before time began," said the Mystic Mullah. "I do not live, even now. I tell you to forget. It would be well for you to heed."

"And if we don't?" Monk asked curiously.

"My slaves, the green souls that are like flying serpents, will come to you," said the Mystic Mullah. "Then you will join me."

Out of the side of his mouth, Monk breathed, "Let's take this nut, whoever he is!"

"Righto!" Ham breathed back.

A string of powder blazes came from Monk's machine pistol. They came so swiftly that they resembled a short, solid red rod, and the noise of the remarkable gun was a tremendous bawl of sound.

The greenish lips writhed and the voice said calmly, "I am not a being who can be killed."

Monk snorted and waited. He was surprised, but still hopeful. His machine pistol fired mercy bullets, hollow shells filled with a drug which caused unconsciousness without doing permanent damage. That was why he had shot. The slugs would not harm the green-faced one to any extent, and they would teach the fellow a lesson.

But nothing happened. The green face remained suspended where it was.

"Dang it!" Monk ripped, and lunged forward.

The green countenance vanished then—simply vanished. It turned slightly as it disappeared, and afterward there was no trace.

Monk fired again. The red blaze from the machine pistol muzzle furnished some light, by which Monk fully expected to see his foe.

His mouth fell open and astonishment came out of his throat in a hacking grunt. There was no one, nothing visible but the brick wall against which the greenish face had been stationed, and on the wall little splashes, wetly glistening, where the mercy bullets had burst.

Ham, lunging in a circle, switched his sword cane. He waved the weapon lightly, so that, if it struck a body, it could cut in only far enough to introduce the stupefying drug. But the blade encountered only the chilly fog and the night.

"Strike a match!" Monk rapped.

Ham did not carry matches, but he produced a jeweled lighter and rasped its tiny flame into being. He cupped it in a palm and turned slowly, throwing the luminance it made.

Fog streamers, crawling past, lent a spookish aspect to the place, but there was no wraith solid enough to be a human body. Out of the harbor, the foghorns still moaned, but the hissing of steam escaping from the near-by tugboat had stopped.

Ham turned his light upward. The warehouse wall reared sheer, unbroken by windows or other openings, for fully thirty feet above them. It was smooth, too smooth for any man to climb.

"He ducked out," Ham said.

Monk started forward, stopped, stared, and made a gesture at his eyes, as if doubting them. He turned, and Ham, who knew the homely chemist as well as any living man, could not remember when he had seen Monk look so awe-stricken.

"Look!" Monk pointed at the ground.

There was pavement underfoot and along the warehouse wall, but winds, strong down here by the river, had swept dust in and banked it shallowly over the bricks. The fog, the occasional drizzles of rain, had wet this dust, turning it into mud which bore their own footprints distinctly.

But below, where the green face had been, there were no footprints; indeed, there was no mark other than the tiny indentations made by fragments of brick which the mercy bullets had chipped off the warehouse wall.

"Blast it!" Monk said. *"Nobody was standing here!"* Monk's voice was hollow.

They stood there, two very startled men, and the chill wind blew out Ham's lighter and he ignited it again, as if not liking the sudden rush of darkness.

Monk wet his lips repeatedly. Their enmity was forgotten; this showed how deeply they were moved, for these two had been known to carry on their perpetual quarrel in the thick of a fight for their lives.

"Blazes!" Monk muttered. "Blazes!"

Ham cleared his throat as if wanting to say something, then did not speak, but raised his lighter again and illuminated their surroundings.

"It was preposterous!" he said.

"Sure," Monk told him slowly. "But explain it. Do that."

"Well——" Ham began, but got no further, hesitated, and finished: "Jove! A confounded mystery if there ever was one!"

"The Mystic Mullah," Monk murmured. "The man who is not a man and who lived a thousand thousand years ago. What a goofy yarn that was."

"The face!" Ham shuddered, dropped his sword cane, then retrieved it. "What an unearthly thing it was."

Monk grasped his arm deliberately and pinched it.

"Snap out of it!" he snorted. "Such things don't happen. There was a trick to it. Let's go on and have a look at that tug, the *Whale of Gotham*."

Ham asked, "What about the warning?"

"Don't make me laugh," Monk growled.

"I suspect it would take quite a bit to make you laugh right now," Ham said grimly.

Monk scowled. "Listen, shyster, you look as if you had just come from a spook interview yourself."

"You hairy ape," Ham said cordially. "How'd you like for me to leave you here—cut in assorted pieces?"

And thus, with their quarrel faintly resumed, and feeling a bit more normal, they moved along the blank side of the warehouse toward the little-used wharf where the tug, *Whale of Gotham*, was moored.

Near by, the waves sobbed; and a flurry of rain arrived with a wet shotting noise, splattering clammily on their hands, their faces.

"Come on!" Monk snapped. "We'll get wet!"

They began to run, but not swiftly, for it was intensely dark and they were without light.

Ham, the more agile on his feet, was in the lead, his hands out before him, seining the darkness. Unexpectedly, he felt a pain across his knuckles. It was a burning sensation as if a red-hot iron had been laid there. The agony stabbed. He exploded in a grunt and recoiled.

"What's wrong?" Monk demanded.

Ham started to answer—but instead, thumbed on his lighter, holding it high. What he saw caused him to howl at the top of his voice.

"Run!" he bellowed.

Monk stood rooted in gape-jawed surprise. He had seen the same thing as Ham—vague, nebulous green things floating in the night. They seemed alive, squirming through the murk like winged serpents. One of the fantastic bodies was afloat near Ham's knuckles.

Monk felt sudden pain, yelled, and knew he had touched one of the green mysteries. He launched a blow, hit nothing, then felt horrible agony scorch his neck.

There was nothing visible, no sound. Monk made snarlings and tried to get his machine pistol out. Again, agony scorched him. It was like an iron at red heat.

Ham was fighting near by. All of his blows fanned air, but often his fists were burned. He lashed with his sword cane. That did no good. He went down. He felt ill, nauseated.

Ham could feel the streaks of agony elsewhere on his lithe body now. There were stabs at his ankles, across his back where his shirt was wet from the rain and from his own perspiration. They were horrible. They brought mad screeches to his lips. Red curtains of agony fluttered before his eyes. It was as if he were being beaten.

Monk tried to get up. He could still hear Ham's mouthings, but they were weaker. It came to the chemist that his own voice was fading. It seemed to go away, to become a thing in the infinite distance.

His last sensation was that his own voice had gone entirely away, leaving him in a silence that was profound, a darkness that was complete.

Chapter 4

THE BRONZE SHADOW

On the tug *Whale of Gotham,* there was tense suspense. The skipper stood with both hands cupped behind his ears, listening. He had heard the cries of Monk and Ham.

The deckhand who had seen Hadim's knife stood near by, also listening.

"Something's up," he said.

"You bet there is!" agreed the skipper. "Where's a lantern? And hand me that signal pistol. I'm gonna investigate."

"That signal pistol won't help much," muttered the deckhand.

"Hell it won't!" The skipper scowled. "Ever see how one of them rocket balls will burn a man?"

He got his lantern and his signal pistol and clambered down out of the pilot house. He was a hard, bold man, this tug captain, and there was no cowardice in his makeup, and not much caution. He approached a spot from which he could leap to the dock.

A tall figure reared up in the lantern light and stood with folded arms. The hook-nosed face was inscrutable; the flowing *abah,* the embroidered *jubbah* and the queer-looking *shirwals* lent the figure an exotic appearance.

The tug skipper, recognizing his passenger, the Khan Nadir Shar, stopped.

"I would not," said the Khan, "go ashore."

"You wouldn't?" growled the captain. "Why not?"

"It would not be advisable," said the Khan, speaking his English that was so perfect it was almost unpleasant.

The skipper put out his jaw and swung his rocket pistol where it showed distinctly in the lantern light. The rocket pistol resembled a single-barreled shotgun sawed off and fitted with a revolver grip.

"Why not?" he repeated.

"I hoped it would not be necessary to tell you this," said the Khan Nadir Shar. "But my life is in danger. So is the life of Joan Lyndell, the American woman who accompanies me. I believe that noise might have been made to decoy you

21

ashore, that you might be put out of the way, leaving us alone and defenseless."

The skipper expanded a little under that. So these people depended on him? That appealed to his fighting instincts.

The Khan Nadir Shar dipped a hand inside his *jubbah* and brought out a big automatic. The tug captain took it. It was an American army gun.

"An extra hundred dollars," promised the Khan, "if you will stand guard, letting no one aboard without first calling me."

The skipper did not consider long. A hundred was a hundred.

"Sure," he said.

The Khan Nadir Shar now went below, walking slowly, as if he had no concern in the world. He did not walk into Joan Lyndell's stateroom this time, but knocked first and spoke softly.

Joan Lyndell was sitting in the same chair, as if she had not moved, and she held her blue automatic precisely as she had before.

"What was it?" she asked.

"The Mystic Mullah, I fear," the Khan said precisely. "I have heard his victims die before. They have a peculiar way of crying out as they feel the touch of the Mystic Mullah's green soul slaves, and their shrieks gradually die away, taking about the same time before——"

"Stop it!" the girl rapped.

The Khan bowed. "Sorry."

Knuckles banged the door.

"Guy out here that says he wants to see you," said the tug skipper's voice. "He looks like a walking skeleton and he just got here."

"What is his name?" the Khan asked precisely.

"Says it's William Harper Littlejohn," said the tug captain.

The Khan Nadir Shar absently traced a hand along the embroidery of his *jubbah*. On his forehead, the serpent design coiled about the jewel seemed to stand out more distinctly than before.

"A William Harper Littlejohn signed the radiogram which came to us at sea," he said. "The message which informed us that Doc Savage was not available for the time being."

Joan Lyndell stood up. She was very tall and there was a regal quality about her.

"Hadim must have delivered his message," she said. "Let this Littlejohn in. He is one of Doc Savage's aides."

The door was opened. The man who came in was very tall, very thin, and had a prominent forehead. His clothes hung upon him as on the lath frame of a scarecrow. In one hand, he juggled a monocle which had a thick lens that was obviously a strong magnifier.

He looked at the Khan Nadir Shar, at the design tattooed on the man's forehead, and he plainly recognized it for what it signified, for he bowed slightly. Then he eyed the girl, and bowed again.

"Where are my associates, Monk and Ham?" he asked.

The Khan said nothing.

Joan Lyndell looked puzzled.

"What do you mean?" she asked.

"Doc Savage was not in town," said the bony man. "I am Johnny, one of his five assistants. Monk and Ham are two more of Doc's men. They came down to see you."

Joan Lyndell held her gun tightly and said, "The noises we heard! The screams!"

The skeleton of a man frowned. "Elucidate, please?" he said.

"Strange noises which might have been shrieks, some minutes ago," said the Khan.

Joan Lyndell asked, "Then Hadim got to you?"

"Hadim?" The tall man stopped juggling the monocle magnifier. "Was he the brown gentleman with the large knife up his sleeve?"

"Was?" The girl lowered her gun. "What do you mean?"

"We found him dead in the corridor, with his neck broken," said the bony man.

A short, sharp whistle came from the Khan. He had jerked breath in through his teeth. Joan Lyndell held her gun tightly at her side and her breathing was audible.

"The Mystic Mullah!" she said hoarsely.

The unnaturally thin man said sharply, "What are you talking about?"

"The Mystic Mullah's victims die from broken necks," the Khan Nadir Shar said precisely.

The bony man waved an arm.

"Wait a minute!" he said. "We'll get all of this straightened out later. Doc Savage came back after Monk and Ham had left. I told him what had happened. He sent me down here to get you all and bring you to him."

"He will help us?" the girl asked eagerly.

"How can he tell?" asked the gaunt man. "He does not know what it is all about."

"But I thought Hadim——"

"Hadim died before he could do more than scratch a clue on the wall which led us down here," replied the bony man. "Will you go with me, please. I will take you to Doc Savage."

The Khan asked, "But what about the other two—Monk and Ham?"

The tall man shrugged. "Doc Savage will know what to do about that."

"We have no luggage," said Joan Lyndell. "Let's go."

The tugboat captain watched them disappear into the night, then looked at the hundred-dollar bill which the Khan had given him. He snapped it in his hands, held it close to the lantern, then looked doubtful, for he had not seen enough hundred-dollar bills to know what they resembled. After that, he made a washing gesture with his hands, as if cleaning them of the whole affair.

The deckhand loomed out of the wet murk.

"Hey, cap," he said. "I think we oughta call the cops and spill this whole thing."

The skipper hastily stowed the greenback.

"Why?" he demanded.

The deckhand came close and spoke in a low voice.

"Just before that long bony guy got here, I thought I'd look around, so I crawled up on the dock," he said. "I eased up alongside a pile of boxes. And boy, did I get an earful! After I listened a minute, I thought I was nuts!"

"What did you hear?" asked the skipper.

Instead of answering, the deckhand said, "Oh!" rather loudly, then another "Oh!" that was even louder. The second "Oh!" was choked up with something.

The skipper lifted his lantern, his eyes protruded and he jumped madly backward. He opened his mouth to bark something having to do with astonishment, but he was so shocked that no sound came forth.

The deckhand was flailing his arms and crying "Oh!" again and again, each time in a more horrible tone. The breath puff of each "Oh!" seemed to distort the hideous green worm of a thing that was rolling against his face, coiling around it, as if caressing it.

The deckhand struck at his own features and his hands, it was quite plain, passed completely through the nebulous green horror, with the result that the verdant thing was separated into two sections, each of which seemed to take on added life and slide over the man's nose.

The deckhand sucked in breath, and one of the green

snakelike things crawled partially inside his mouth, then hastily out again. The deckhand shrieked more hoarsely and fell flat on his face, where his squirmings became rapidly less, and his head began to bend backward strangely, as if something invisible, some unseen master of strength, had gripped his neck.

The skipper was yelling now, striking with his lantern at one of the green bodies in the air in front of him. He succeeded in fanning it away with his lantern, but stepped backward directly into another of the citrine horrors. He shrieked; and jumping away, slipped and banged his lantern down, batting its flame out and extinguishing it.

After that, there was intense darkness, out of which came unearthly and sickening sounds of a man making a rendezvous with death.

In the midst of the other sounds there was a hollow crack, as if some one had broken a stick of candy while it was still wrapped in its paper covering. A bit later, there was another crack, almost identical; and after that, there was silence except for the bubbling suck of waves and the far-away foghorns.

For perhaps the span of a minute, the quiet held.

A light appeared. It was a weird beam, thin as a white string, and it laced about with eerie speed until it found the two forms on the tug deck.

Both skipper and deckhand lay with postures grotesquely distorted, their heads bent back in a manner which indicated with certainty that their necks were broken. There was no sign of the nebulous green monstrosities.

The thin, white beam of light collapsed suddenly. Quiet again gripped the vicinity, except for the small sounds of the water, which were sufficient to cover other minor noises. A wave nudged the tug into the dock, and the fenders screamed out like condemned souls, as they ground between hull planking and dock spiles.

There was no sound of anything living, no trace that the wielder of the thin-beamed flashlight had moved; yet inshore, toward the end of the dock, where there was a little glow reflected from a distant street light, a shadow moved unexpectedly. It was a very large shadow and quite shapeless, with nothing definite enough about it to identify it.

A bit later, the shadowy figure materialized again, some distance down the street, near where three other figures stood.

The other three figures were Joan Lyndell, the Khan Nadir

Shar, and the skeleton-thin man with the magnifying monocle. They were close under a street lamp, hugging it as if its brilliance were an actual protection.

Joan Lyndell was saying, "I think we had better go back."

The Khan shivered. He looked scared.

"I do not know what we should do," he said.

The bony man exhaled noisily as if trying to relax from an unpleasant tension. He jerked his head.

"The thing to do is get you two to Doc Savage," he said sharply. "Let Doc get hold of this thing."

"We have come half around the world to do that very thing," murmured the girl. "But something happened back at the tug. I could hear it."

And the bony man snapped, "We're not going back. Come on!"

They advanced, the skeleton of a man now using a flashlight. The beam soon picked up a car, a large sedan. The thin man got behind the wheel and put the machine into motion.

It was raining again, cold, bitter drops which ran over the car top with sounds like small-footed unseen things. The windshield wiper began to *swick-swuck* monotonously. They passed through streets that were like the avenues of the dead, for none were abroad in the rain.

The sedan covered many blocks, but did not get over in the theatrical district with its tinsel blaze. When the machine stopped finally, it was before a gloomy structure that resembled a shabby factory building. The headlight glow, splashing sidewise, revealed a "To Rent" sign which looked old.

The bony man got from behind the wheel, came around and opened the rear door adjacent to the curb. He leaned far inside and switched on the dome light.

A blue revolver was disclosed in his hand. It shifted its menace from the Khan to the girl.

"Think it over," the skeleton man advised. "The boss said to kill you if you got funny."

The Khan choked, "Then Doc Savage——"

"Doc Savage—hell!" the other said harshly. "I've never even seen Doc Savage!"

The girl said in a small dry voice, "Then you——"

"I'm doing this job for the Mystic Mullah," the skeleton man told her. "Get out! Go inside! And no——"

The bony man fell silent.

He was silent because of a sound. A sound that had come

into existence so gradually that it had at first not been noticed. The sound was still vague, but it was real, so real that it possessed a quality of menace, of promised events.

It was a trilling. It traced a fantastic musical scale, rising and falling, but not repeating its notes or indicating in any way that it adhered to a definite tune. It was low, nearly impossible of description. It might have been the product of a chill wind through the fog, or the song of some exotic tropical bird. And it was entirely unnatural, awe-inspiring.

The skeleton-thin man glared at the Khan and the girl. There was nothing to show from whence the weird sound came, but he thought one of them was making it.

"Cut it out!" he snarled. "Get out of there and pile into this old factory!"

He stepped back. Then he convulsed violently. His gun dropped from his hand. He tried to cry out, but his mouth, open at its widest, emitted no sound. He twisted around, staring, seeming not to understand what had happened to him.

Only when he got his head around was he aware of the giant form which had floated soundlessly out of the fog and fastened upon him. The giant was a man, but he seemed huge beyond all human proportions. Maybe the fog helped that impression, the fog and the incredible strength of the mighty hand which held his neck in a paralyzing clutch, and the other hand which, gripping his arm, had twisted and caused the gun to fall.

The giant dropped the gun in a coat pocket. He seemed unhurried. His free hand went to the thin man's neck and did something to nerve centers. The man became tense, as if seized with a spell that he could not break, and when he was released, he fell to the slimy sidewalk and did not move, except to roll his eyes in horror.

The giant stepped close to the car and the dome light showed his features. They were features of an amazing regularity. But the handsomeness of the big man's face did not make it distinctive. It was his bronze hue; his countenance might have been moulded from metal. Too, it was his eyes, like pools of flake-gold stirred by tiny winds. Weird eyes, they seemed possessed of a compelling power, an ability to literally convey orders with their glance.

The bronze man wore no head covering, and his hair, of a bronze hue only slightly darker than his skin, lay smooth and unruffled as a metallic skullcap. His neck was bundled with fantastic sinews, and the tendons on the backs of his bronze hands were of unnatural size.

The girl, Joan Lyndell, had her blue automatic out, but she did not lift it. Instead, she spoke throatily.

"You are Doc Savage," she told the bronze man.

The remarkable bronze man did not reply. He studied the pair in the sedan. Then he made a small gesture at the skeleton man so weirdly paralyzed on the sidewalk.

When he spoke, his voice was in keeping with his striking appearance, a voice that was deep and cultivated, conveying the impression that it was capable of great flexibility.

"This man told you he was Johnny—William Harper Littlejohn?" he asked.

"Isn't he?" the girl countered.

"No," said the bronze man. "He has made himself up to look something like Johnny."

The Khan Nadir Shar seemed to have been beyond speech. Now he reached up and absently touched the design tattooed on his forehead; that seemed to awaken him.

"You are—Doc Savage," he said precisely. "How did you get here?"

"I have been away," the bronze man said simply. "A short while ago, I returned to my headquarters and learned that Monk and Ham, two of my aides, had gone to the tug. My arrival there was simultaneous with your own departure. I followed you."

The girl said rapidly, "Something happened back at the tug shortly after we left. Do you have any idea what it was?"

"I heard the sounds," admitted the bronze man. "I went back and used a flashlight. Two men, apparently the skipper of the tug and one of his deckhands, were dead. Their necks seemed to be broken. There was not time to investigate thoroughly, because it was necessary to follow you."

"The Mystic Mullah!" the girl said hoarsely. "His green soul slaves!"

Doc Savage studied her, his metallic features inscrutable.

"What makes you say that?" he asked.

"The Mystic Mullah's victims always die with their necks broken," replied the girl. "The green soul slaves—do that."

The Khan Nadir Shar knotted and unknotted his hands and his jeweled finger rings ground together softly.

"The Mystic Mullah is here!" he moaned. "His green soul slaves will find us! They go everywhere——" He fell silent.

Doc Savage continued to study them. His flake-gold eyes, catching the glow from the dome light, gave the impression of being strangely luminous.

"This will all have to be explained," he said. "But first, our friend here will talk."

The bronze man stepped back and picked up the skeleton-thin man. He did something to the nerve centers near the fellow's neck, and the man regained the use of his limbs as if by magic. He tried to fight, but he was battered against the car with a fierce roughness and held so helpless that he began to whimper.

"Where is the Mystic Mullah?" Doc Savage asked.

The victim stared, moaned as the bronze hands hurt him more, then seemed to reach a sudden conclusion that it would be wise to tell what he knew.

"I don't know," he groaned. "Listen; I wouldn't have gone into this if I had known I would have to buck you, Savage. I've heard of you, see. I'm an actor. A ham. I've been having it tough.

"A guy telephones me and asks me will I go to the tug and get these two people, tell them my story, and bring them here. I get two hundred for the job. I never seen the guy who hired me, see. He left a picture at my hotel and telephoned me to make up like the picture. The picture's in my pocket."

Doc Savage dipped a hand inside the man's coat and brought out a piece of cardboard to which was pasted a newspaper cutout of William Harper Littlejohn, the eminent archæologist and geologist.

"The guy on the telephone said you were out of town and would never know," moaned the bony man. "What a sucker I was!"

Doc Savage watched the man steadily, making the other return his stare, turning the other's face when he sought to avoid the menace of the fantastic flake-gold eyes.

The thin man squirmed and more and more horror came upon his cadaverous face; his tongue swabbed over his lips, but it was dry and left no wetness, and his eyelids rolled back until most of the eyeballs showed.

"I told you the truth!" he shrieked suddenly. "What are you going to do with me?"

The nature of the answer, if there was an answer intended, was never known, for a voice shrilled out suddenly from the depths of the grimy old factory building.

"Don't!" it screamed. "Get those things off me!"

It was Monk's voice.

Chapter 5

AFTER MONK YELLED

The skeleton-thin man barked out in agony as Doc Savage slammed him into the sedan. He floundered down on the floorboards at the feet of the girl and the Khan Nadir Shar, and lay there, stunned.

"Two blocks north, one west," Doc rapped. "Drive there and wait for me!"

The girl, comprehending instantly, scrambled out of the rear door and into the front one, inserting her slender form behind the wheel.

The Khan began, "But who—what the——"

"That was Monk, one of my men," said the bronze man. "Watch this ham actor here. He knows more than he has told us, if his manner is any indication."

The Khan removed an automatic from under his *jubbah*. It was a thin-snouted foreign weapon which fired a bullet with the penetration force of some rifles. He put the snout against the temple of the bony prisoner.

"Be careful," Doc warned.

"Your warning is not necessary," the Khan said, his English still unnaturally perfect. "We well know the hideous power of this Mystic Mullah."

It was doubtful if the bronze man heard the last of that, for he had faded into the fog and wet darkness. He went directly to the entrance of the warehouse, but did not touch the door, which was closed. He paused there, entirely immobile.

He was using his ears, organs which had been developed by years of scientific treatment and exercise until they had a sensitivity that was far beyond the normal. There were sounds inside, low and uneven, as if something were rubbing against something else with short strokes.

The bronze man did not touch the door, or go closer. He moved away. Those sounds were made by men waiting on the other side of the panel, men who were trying not to breathe loudly, and as a result, made occasional strained gasps.

The bronze man searched in the darkness, found a ledge

on the face of the building where mortar had weathered out, and lifted himself up. A projecting window ledge furnished his next grip. He used a handkerchief to wipe off the damp stone. The city grime, soaked with the fog and rain, made a paste only slightly less slick than grease.

He tried the window. Glass was gone from it. Inside, there were boards planked over.

Down in the street, the sedan departed, making very little noise.

The bronze giant set himself on the window ledge and struck a sudden, violent blow. The impact seemed more than human knuckles could withstand. He struck again instantly. The plank split, caved, and he grasped the edges and wrenched it out; then, although the adjacent boards were nearly three quarters of an inch thick, he tore them aside as if they had been shingles.

The crash of wood, the scream of nails drawing, echoed through the old structure. There were other sounds, too. Men were running on the stairs. Voices were shouting.

The language they spoke was the gobbling, clucking dialect—weird to the unaccustomed ear—common to certain remote areas of central Asia.

Then lights burst into the room, white-hot, stingings rods of brilliance from powerful flashlights. A man babbled out in the strange language. Then powder roar slammed and plaster, loosened by a bullet, ran off the wall in a gray stream.

The bullet missed Doc Savage. He was far to the left when it struck.

The room was enormous. Humped here and there over the floor were foundations for heavy machinery. A few still supported bulky machines. They were like a forest, and excellent shelter.

The bronze man got down behind the machine foundations. Instead of continuing to the left, he went straight ahead. The attackers were cackling profanely in their dialect. A moment later, Doc Savage saw one of them. A switching flash beam outlined him distinctly.

The man was wolfishly lean, with very black hair and eyes, the latter with the merest of slants, and his skin was the color of a gunnysack. He was clad immaculately in clothing which would not draw a second glance on New York streets.

He carried a thin-nosed automatic, similar to the one produced by the Khan Nadir Shar. The weapon could drive a slug through half a dozen human bodies.

Doc saw others of the attacking party a moment later;

and they were similar in appearance to the first. Central Asiatics, all of them, men from a land where life was cheap.

Alert, deadly, they prowled the big room, spreading out, twisting the heads of their flashlights to cause them to throw wider beams. Some fell back to watch the stairway and the door.

It was toward these latter that Doc Savage directed his attention. Monk and Ham were here somewhere. Finding them was the bronze man's goal. And it would have to be accomplished by some means other than brute force, or an open gun fight, for Doc carried no firearms.

He never carried a gun. He had a specific reason for this, maintaining that a man who carried a firearm came to depend upon it; and once it was taken from him, that man would tend to feel completely helpless.

The bronze man touched rusty lengths of iron. They were bolts, heavy things, piled together. He raised up with one of them and threw it. His target was not one of the men at the door, but one on the far side of the large room. He did not want them to think he was near the door. The bolt struck the victim between thigh and knee and he screamed and fell down.

Instantly, there was a rush for the spot. They thought the man must have been struck at close range, not realizing the ability of the bronze man's great muscles to throw far and accurately.

From below, downstairs and to the rear, a voice bellowed out. It was Monk again.

"Watch out, Doc!" he howled. "They made me yell that first time to draw you inside! I didn't know that!"

The bronze man knew it now. His discovery of the waiting men behind the door downstairs, had told him it was a trap. He scuttled swiftly, taking advantage of the uproar at the other end of the room.

A dark-skinned man sighted him, let out a yell. The cry choked off suddenly as a heavy bolt glanced from the man's head to the wall. Man and bolt hit the floor together.

Gunshots *whoom-whoomed!* in the cavernous room. Lead clanged on machinery or slapped the walls fiercely. But Doc Savage was already at the stairs. He went down swiftly, reached the bottom, took a step forward—and stopped.

A light gushed. It was not a bright, blinding light, but a mellow one, designed not to blind. It came from the head of a flashlight which someone had wrapped in a single thickness of handkerchief.

The light was brilliant enough to reveal four slant-eyed

brown faces, their very inscrutability something terrible. Each of the men held one of the spike-nosed guns. But to these had been fitted ram's-horn magazines, and the gears in the mechanism were no doubt filed so that the guns were continuously automatic in operation, capable of emptying thirty or so shots in a single blast.

"*Wallah!*" one rasped in his native tongue. "It would be good to take this bronze devil alive, that we might show the Mystic Mullah we are sons of the mountain fox."

Doc Savage stood very still. The next word would decide his fate.

"It is a good thought," agreed another of the four.

The four men came close. They held their doctored automatics at waist level, gripping them with both hands. This showed they knew what they were doing. Only an inexperienced man will try to fire an automatic altered so that it discharges as long as the trigger is held back, for the recoil will kick such a weapon up, possibly blowing out the brains of an unwary individual.

The gun snouts pressed hard against the bronze man. Hands reached out, ripped his pockets open, spilling the contents, and slapped places where weapons might be concealed.

"His muscles are as hard as the rock walls of Tanan," murmured one of the party in his strange language. "Watch him closely. He must have terrible strength."

Doc Savage asked, "Why do you seek my life?"

The gun muzzles jiggled against his side as the men started. They were surprised, for the bronze giant had spoken their mother language as perfectly as they themselves.

"It was not an idly wagging tongue that said this man knows all things," one of the four muttered. "Even in Asia, few men speak our tongue as well as he does."

"It is said that the man who faces danger quietly lives to face it again," said another. "He is too calm. Watch him closely."

Men began coming down the stairs. They cackled in their excitement. Those who had been hurt were helped by others.

The man who had given orders upstairs faced Doc Savage and showed black teeth. He did not speak at once, but slowly prepared a chew of betel nut, the ingredients for which he drew from a pocket of his neat business suit. The chewing of betel had made his teeth black. He watched closely; and discovering no trace of fear on the bronze giant's features, seemed disgusted.

"A wise man knows when to be frightened," he said.

"There can be fear without shaking and wailing," Doc Savage said in the tongue of Tanan.

"You are a strange one," said the man in English. "I can understand why the Mystic Mullah should come from the other side of the world to dispose of you before you heard the story of the Khan Shar and the white woman, Joan Lyndell."

"I am curious about this Mystic Mullah," the bronze man stated quietly. "Who is he?"

"He was dead and sat for a thousand years in one spot, thinking," the other said matter of factly. "He knows all things and can do all things. After he had meditated, he detached his spirit from himself and sent it to earth, to Tanan, to enlighten men and lead them to their proper destiny."

"You," Doc Savage told him, "sound like a coolie who has partaken too freely of the product of the poppy."

The other smiled fiercely. "The Mystic Mullah is greater than the Genghis Khan, greater even than Allah, or Buddha. Beside him, Confucius was as the child scholar who puzzles over his first books. These things, you will learn."

"Here in America, they have a word for such talk," said the bronze man.

"What is it?"

"Hokum!" answered the bronze man.

All of the men were down from upstairs now. They had gathered in a close ring. None of them had faces of morons. Rather, their features were those of intelligent men. But they were also the faces of killers, men who took life for a purpose they considered right and just.

"Watch!" rapped the bronze man.

He lifted both hands above his head, began to knot and unknot the fingers in a slow, fantastic fashion.

"Stop it!" grated the chief of the brown-skinned men. His eyes were on Doc's hands. So were the eyes of his companions. They could not understand it.

Nor did Doc expect them to understand. The strange movements of his hands were simply to draw their attention from his feet as he stepped on one heel with the toe of the other foot and strained. The heel of his shoe was dislodged so easily that it was evident it was equipped with some type of hinge. A yellowish powder spilled out, making a small mound on the floor.

Doc stepped back, turned half around, put his hands over his face and bent double.

There was a terrific, eye-hurting white light. A *plop* of sound accompanied it, not unlike the setting off of a photographer's flash light gun. The light burned for perhaps a full two seconds, dense white smoke pouring from the mound of powder. The light went out.

Only then did guns begin going off.

It was too late. Doc Savage had lunged with the first burst of light. He knew what would happen. The chemical mixture was infinitely stronger than magnesium; it made a light so strong that it produced almost complete blindness for a few moments. The stuff was ignited by a small pellet of another chemical compound which burst into flame shortly after it was exposed to the air.

The brown men milled about, cursing in their dialect. Fully twenty shots were fired wildly. Two men fell, knocked down by the bullets of their fellows.

Doc Savage did not linger, or try to make any capture. The blindness would not last long enough for that. It was momentary, as if a flashlight had been splashed into eyes accustomed to intense darkness.

The bronze man moved toward the rear. It was from there that Monk's yell had come. He found an open door. It gave into an alley.

On the alley pavement were tracks, faintly discernible in the fog slime. Doc followed them, and came out on a street. The tracks crossed a sidewalk. Recently, there had been work done on the street pavement, necessitating the use of sand, and a film of the stuff still remained.

Doc Savage knew the footprint sizes of Monk and Ham. He found them both. Monk had a peculiar shambling gait and large feet. Ham's shoes were small, almost feminine, and he put his feet down straight, without toeing in or out. The tracks ended on the sidewalk. Across the curb there were other marks, made by automobile tires. These were still practically dry, the moisture having been forced aside by the weight of the car. The machine had left only a moment ago. It must have had a quiet engine not to be heard inside the abandoned factory.

The brown men of Tanan were yelling; some dashed out and splattered their flashlights in the alley, then came running toward where Doc stood.

The bronze man faded away into the damp night. He reached the main thoroughfare, turned north two blocks, then went one west. It was there that the Khan Nadir Shar and the girl should have waited in the sedan.

Doc found the sedan. It was dark, with the headlights and

the dome light extinguished. He stopped a few yards away, listened, then went on. He did not call out. He splashed his own flash beam into the machine.

There was only a body inside, a body with a twisted, grotesquely broken neck. It was the skeleton-thin man who had claimed he was a ham actor hired to play the part of William Harper Littlejohn.

Of the Khan Nadir Shar and Joan Lyndell there was no trace.

Chapter 6

THE RESCUED MAN

Doc Savage looked the sedan over closely, noting engine and license numbers, the make of the tires, the location of the inevitable dents in the fenders. Probably it was a stolen machine.

Down the street, the brown-skinned Tananese were pushing a speedy search. In the distance, a police siren was making uproar; it seemed to come closer, an indication that the shooting inside the abandoned factory had attracted attention.

The Tananese apparently heard the siren, but were so unfamiliar with American life that they failed to realize what it was until the very closeness of the eerie whine told them it was bound for this spot. Then they scattered, scuttling away like frightened rats.

Doc Savage himself eased away. He wished to learn more about the Mystic Mullah before giving any information to the police. A moment later, the bronze man reached his roadster.

It was a long car, manufactured by a concern noted for the long life of its machines. It would take an experienced observer to tell that the machine was armor-plated.

Seating himself behind the wheel, Doc Savage drew on a peculiar looking pair of overgrown goggles. The lenses of these were considerably larger but of the same shape as condensed milk cans. He shifted tiny switches on the goggle affair and they began to make a faint whizzing. This was barely audible.

Doc next flicked a switch on the dash. To one standing near by, it would have seemed that nothing happened. Certainly no visible lights came on.

But to Doc Savage, wearing the strange goggles, a stretch ahead of the car had become illuminated with an unearthly distinctness. It was not like ordinary light, this luminance. Objects stood out in stark high lights and shadows and there was no sense of color. It was as if everything had taken on varied shades of black and white.

The effect was produced by an infraray projector mounted forward of the hood. The infra-light was ordinarily invisible to the unaided eye, and its use in headlights was made possible only by the intricate goggles which the bronze man wore.

It was by use of this invisible light that the bronze man had been able to follow the girl and the Khan Nadir Shar.

The roadster ran with the silence of a ghost through the darkened streets, wheeled to the left and sought an even more secluded district.

It was raining again, another of the brief flurries which had been prevalent all evening. The wet drops, striking the bronze man's uncovered head, ran off with the peculiar effect of water shedding from the back of a water-fowl. The rain seemed to bother him not at all.

He clicked switches concealed under the dash, and a radio loud-speaker began to spew metallic static. From a concealed hook, the bronze man lifted a microphone, a sensitive instrument with an enclosing mouthpiece so constructed that, by holding it close to the lips, one could speak without bystanders hearing.

"Any luck?" he asked, then listened to the radio speaker.

"Plenty," said a rather nasal voice. "Drive across Queensborough Bridge and turn north through Astoria."

Doc Savage swung the roadster about, complying with the directions. He kept to secluded streets and broke the speed limit steadily, except on the upper level across the bridge, when he was limited by the speed of the other cars in the double traffic lane, there being no room for passing.

He was nearly across the bridge when the nasal voice came out of the radio speaker again.

"An old refinery on the river," it said. "We're waiting for you at the beginning of the lane that leads to the refinery."

The lane was narrow, rutted deeply by trucks, but it did not look as if it had been used much recently. There was high brush alongside it, brush from which the leaves had fallen, for the season was well in the Fall. Although it was comparatively warm now, snow had fallen briefly weeks before.

The man who stepped out in front of the roadster was thin, somewhat scrawny, and he had a complexion which was, as far as appearances went, strikingly unhealthy. He looked as if he had grown up in a cellar with mushrooms. He had the color of a mushroom.

The unhealthy-looking man came close to the roadster and said, "They turned into that old refinery, Doc. I don't think it's being used. They must have bought off the watchman."

Doc Savage said, "Good work, Long Tom."

The pallid man was Major Thomas J. Roberts. He looked vaguely like a corpse, but he could whip three times his weight in ordinary men. Furthermore, he was a wizard in the field of electricity, a genius of the "juice."

Another man lumbered out of the night, a tower of gristle and bone almost as large as Doc Savage. He had a long face which wore an expression of utter gloom. He looked as if he had just lost a very dear friend. But the striking thing about the newcomer was his fists. They were incredibly huge, each composed of somewhat more than a quart of bone and sinew.

"Johnny went on ahead to scout around," he said, and his voice, although he tried to keep it down, was like the rumble of an angry lion.

The big-fisted man was Colonel John Renwick, and his name was one known widely in the engineering profession, a trade at which he had made several fortunes. Renny, as he was ordinarily called, was, along with the pallid Long Tom, a member of Doc Savage's group of five unusual aides.

Doc Savage guided the roadster off the lane, parking it in a spot where it was not likely to be seen. Then they all went on ahead.

Johnny met them shortly, a thin lath of darker shadow in the damp fog and darkness. When he spoke, he used his big words.

"Conceivably, could these Orientals conjecture the hypothesis of our pervasion of this circumambiency?"

Renny looked more gloomy.

"Holy cow!" he grumbled. "Don't you ever speak English? Somebody translate that."

Long Tom said sourly, "He means that he wonders if them brown guys could be wise that Doc Savage had us posted in the background at that old factory, so that we could trail them."

"Rats!" said Renny. "Why didn't he say so? I don't think they are wise."

"Did you see what happened to the girl and the king after they drove off in the sedan?" Doc asked.

"King!" Renny exploded.

"The man wears, tattooed on his forehead, the Sacred Seal of Tanan, the mark of the Son of Divinity, Destined Master of Ten Thousand Lances, Ruler of Outer Mongolia," Doc told them.

"Sounds big," said Renny, nodding.

"It means he is absolute ruler of Tanan, possibly the strangest and most medieval city of Asia," Doc replied. "What happened to him and to the girl?"

"They were seized by the brown fellows while waiting in the sedan," Renny replied. "We did not get there in time to prevent it. We heard squawling and pitching around, and got there to find that bony fellow lying dead with what looked like a broken neck. Say, just what happened to him, anyway?"

"The hand of the Mystic Mullah," Doc said.

"Huh?" Renny blinked. "I don't get this."

Doc Savage told them what he had seen and heard, and what had happened. He missed few details, yet his recital was not wordy.

"Holy cow!" Renny mumbled when he finished. "I still don't get it."

"As things happened," Doc replied, "there was no time to hear the story of the Khan and the girl."

The men continued forward and soon could smell the crude tang of the refinery. The odor was not a fresh, gaseous one of oil distilling, but an older, stale one that wafted from grease-soaked earth and disused stills. They came to a high fence, constructed of wire so coarse that it was like iron bars.

They stood listening; and there was no sound, except those that came distantly from the bay. Then an elevated train moaned in the distance.

"Wait here," Doc said.

Surmounting the fence did not present the bronze man with much difficulty. Renny and the others heard the wire groan a little, as he descended the other side of the fence, but after that there was no trace of his progress. It seemed darker than before, and he was almost instantly lost in the moist void.

Doc Savage traveled swiftly, but not so rapidly as to invite mishap. Only the fact that he was feeling out the ground in front of him prevented Doc from falling into an abandoned water-cooling pit.

Shortly after that he saw lights. They were furtive and bobbing, the splash of flashlights used in a cautious manner. He made for them, and soon could see the source of the luminous dabs.

Men were working with large wrenches alongside a bank of pressure stills. They were removing one of the manhole covers, held in place with powerful bolts.

One brown fellow, directing the work, seemed more worldly-wise than the others.

"It is a good prison," he said in the Tananese dialect. "The steel is thick, and their loudest shouts will not be heard."

The last bolt came free, after which they pried off the oval slab of steel which closed the tall metal cylinder. The spokesman thrust his head and a flashlight inside and looked it over.

"It is well," he said. "Go bring the prisoners."

A brown man of Tanan darted away, using his flashlight to avoid the stanchions of aërial pipelines, gate houses and the other rusted appurtenances of the refinery. He lifted the beam eventually and splashed it upon a large brick building. He made directly for the door.

Then a giant of bronze descended upon him, a long-fingered hand of fantastic strength cupping over his mouth and closing in all sound. A single, short blow chopped down, and the messenger became unconscious.

After he had struck down the man, Doc Savage moved to the door of the brick building. The lock, he discovered by the sense of touch, had been torn off. A certain slight sharpness about the ruptured wood fibres indicated that the tearing had been done recently.

The bronze man did not try to enter by the door, but moved to the left, where a window had unexpectedly whitened from a light within. He peered through the window.

The room inside was shabby, with dust and paper on the floor. It did not look as if it had been used for months, bearing out the general impression that the refinery had been closed down for some time.

Several brown Tananese were present. All, after the manner of Orientals in the clothing of Occidentals, looked very neat, rather unnaturally prim.

A stoop-shouldered white man in greasy overalls stood in the center of the room. A metal plate affixed to his greasy cap read, "Night Watchman." He was nervous.

"I'm taking a big chance," he grumbled, and his words carried faintly to Doc Savage.

"You are well paid for letting us use this spot for hiding our prisoners," one of the Tananese told him.

More brown men now appeared, coming from another room. They dragged the apish Monk and the slender, dapperly clad Ham. The two prisoners were bound tightly at the wrists. Ham had managed to retain his attire in a remarkably unruffled condition. The crease in his trousers had a knifelike sharpness.

One of the brown men brought ordinary burlap bags. Monk kicked and struggled, but was unable to prevent one of the bags being drawn over his head and tied at the bottom. Then Ham received the same treatment.

Monk squawled, "You blasted heathen, what're you gonna do with us?"

"Shut up, you furry mistake!" Ham directed at Monk. "The fact that they don't want us to see where we are, shows they're not planning to kill us at once."

Doc Savage ducked suddenly, with all the speed of which he was capable.

The window glass broke, jangling. Flashing steel traveled on through the pane, passed under one of the brown men who jumped into the air with remarkable alacrity, and stuck, quivering, in the baseboard. It was a knife, very heavy of blade.

The sound which had warned Doc Savage was faint; the rasp of cloth as the knife arm was drawn back for the throw. The assailant was undoubtedly a guard who had stood there in the night. The bronze man's sensitive ears would have caught the approach of any one. The fellow must have thrown at the outline of Doc's head against the window.

Once down on all fours, Doc whipped along the building wall. A flashlight popped a white disk on the bricks. This skidded about, located Doc.

"*Ya!*" the knife thrower bawled. "It is the bronze one!"

Doc spotted half a brick in the flash glow, seized it and shied it at the light. The beam vanished in blackness.

"*Ya!*" snarled the brown man. He had not been hit.

Inside the brick building, undoubtedly the refinery office, there was a hollow squabble of shouting. Over toward the pressure still more voices howled. Lights were popping out everywhere, scudding their beams like frightened ghosts.

The night watchman, who had certainly taken a bribe to allow the brown men to hide their prisoners at the refinery, dashed out into the moist night.

"Be quiet!" he squawled. "Somebody'll hear this racket!"

From the direction of the main gate, shot sound came slamming. Hysterical yells followed it. A voice roared like an angry lion in a cave. Renny's voice! Aided by Long Tom and Johnny, he was trying to get into the refinery grounds.

Doc Savage haunted the shadows, skirting the office building in an endeavor to get to Monk and Ham. The Khan Nadir Shar and the girl, Joan Lyndell, if they were alive, might possibly have been brought here also.

Inside the office building, orders cracked in guttural Tananese. After that, the brown men began to move in an orderly manner. They had been searching; now they gave up the hunt and assembled in a compact group about the door.

One of the Orientals dragged a large bag into view, opened it, and started passing out extremely modern and compact gas masks. It was apparent that only two or three of the Tananese had the least idea of how to don these. But amid much profane exchange of directions, they managed to get them on.

Doc Savage had worked close and had drawn from his clothing a number of small glass bulbs filled with a colorless liquid. These were gas bombs capable of producing quick unconsciousness. He returned them to the padded metal case from which they had been removed. Their anæsthetic vapor content was effective only when inhaled; the gas masks had made them useless.

Instead of the gas bombs Doc produced two small cans, each fitted with a screw valve. He opened these valves. The small canisters began making faint hissing sounds.

The bronze man tossed one of the cans toward the brown men, but was careful that it did not roll close enough to come to their attention. The second can he threw very hard, so that it passed entirely over them and landed beyond.

Judging accurately the time it would hit, he yelled loudly to cover the sound of its landing.

The yell brought bullets which snapped like vicious, unseen teeth and climbed away into the night with piercing squeals. Doc lunged over and got behind a nest of pipe gates. A lead slug, hitting the gates, splashed like a hard-driven raindrop.

"Somebody'll hear the noise!" screamed the watchman. "Stop it!"

Two of the brown men consulted in low voices. Then one ran over, stood close in front of the watchman and said something that Doc Savage did not hear. The other brown man came up, unnoticed, behind the watchman.

Doc Savage called loudly, "Watchman—*look out!*"

He was too late, because the slant-eyed brown man behind the watchman leaned forward suddenly with all of his weight, holding both hands clasped in front of his chest. From the knob of his hands protruded the steel thorn of a knife blade, and this disappeared its full length in the watchman's back.

The watchman's scream blew scarlet through his teeth; he fell down heavily, jerked convulsively, then lay on his face while a fountain of red jumped above his back a few times. This stopped as his heart became quiet.

"We can no longer use this place," said one of the

Tananese. "And this white devil ghost"—pointing to the dead watchman—"might have told that which would give us trouble."

Men came running from the direction of the gate. Brown fellows, they sprinted with frenzied speed, squawking that a white devil ghost who was all hands was pursuing them, along with a skeleton that lived and fought terribly, and another man who looked as if he were dead. That would be Renny, Johnny and Long Tom.

Things happened swiftly. A supermachine pistol hooted in the hands of one of Doc's men. That caused the flashlights to go out. Tananese shouts indicated the prisoners were being hauled out of the building.

The brown men came directly toward Doc Savage, and the bronze giant, instead of retreating, found the stanchion which supported an overhead pipeline and climbed. Rust ground under his palms. He balanced atop the pipe.

The brown men began to pass under him. Their breathing was heavy. One fell down; others swore at him. Then they splattered a flashlight beam to see their way.

By the backglow from the light Doc Savage made out the vague forms of prisoners, their heads hooded in gunnysacks so as to prevent them sighting their surroundings. He counted three of the captives, but not all of the party was illuminated. The flash went out.

Doc Savage launched himself headlong into the cluster of Tananese.

The slant-eyed men were naturally expectant of an attack. But they were not ready for it from above. One man, on whose shoulders Doc managed to land, went down; there was a muffled crunch, as a bone broke in some part of him.

Doc kept down, striking upward, wrenching at legs. Men fell heavily. They shrieked; and one not knowing Orientals would have thought they were thinking only of escape. On the contrary, they unsheathed knives and stabbed about with no great consideration for their companions.

Feet pounded as Renny, Long Tom and Johnny came up. They were cautious enough, however, not to display flashlights.

Doc Savage swept a figure from his feet. It was intensely dark. Doc reached for his victim's face. His fingers encountered coarse cloth—a burlap bag. It was one of the prisoners.

The bronze man was near the fringe of the fighting brown men now. He lunged, holding the prisoner, and got clear, then gave the hooded captive a hard shove, propelling him away in the murk. Whirling, Doc plunged into the fight.

But the brown men had recovered from their surprise, had grouped themselves, and were retreating. They brought flashlights into play, along with guns.

Doc, finding himself lodged in a glaring flash beam, whipped for shelter. The only haven in sight was an upright of concrete which supported an overhead pipeline. He got behind it. Fragments began to fall off as bullets smashed.

Renny and the others were also forced back. They used their supermachine pistols, but the brown men got behind a still house, ran from there to abandoned benzine tanks and, in full flight, plunged on past a row of crude tanks.

Renny had a flashlight, and hearing the prisoner whom Doc had rescued emit a groan, switched the beam in that direction. The spike of white picked up a pair of immaculately trousered legs. The rest of the rescued one lay behind a gate box.

"It's Ham!" Renny thundered. "I'd know his clothes anywhere."

They did not wait, but lunged in pursuit of the Tananese. The latter greatly outnumbered them. Doc and his men, in order not to show their position, refrained from using their flashlights. This slowed them up.

They could hear clanking of metal. The men of Tanan must be breaking open a side gate. A moment later, automobile engines whooped into life; headlights jumped out in long funnels and began to move.

"Had cars waiting there for a getaway!" Renny boomed.

Doc and his men reached the gate. They launched a few mercy bullets from the machine pistols, but as far as they could see, got no results.

Long Tom snapped, "I'll get our car and try to follow them!" and started away.

"No use!" Doc cried after him. "You could not pick up their trail!"

Long Tom came back reluctantly, and they reëntered the grounds of the closed refinery. Going back over the back trail of the brown men, they hoped to find some who had been overcome by the mercy bullets. There was no trace of victims.

"Those babies kept their heads," Renny grumbled reluctantly. "They carried off those who got laid out."

"Let us hold interlocution with Ham," suggested bigworded Johnny.

They came soon to the prisoner whom Doc had rescued. The fellow was tumbling about, endeavoring to free his hands. He had not yet been able to remove the gunnysack hood which was over his head.

"It's Ham, all right," Long Tom declared. "Hey, Ham, what'd you learn about them brown eggs? What's behind all of this?"

The hooded man made hacking sounds.

"Gagged," Renny thumped.

The big-fisted engineer bent down, tried to untie the knots in the string which held the gunnysack, had trouble, then calmly gripped the sack with his two huge fists and tore it wide open. He laid the two halves back from the rescued one's face.

Renny was hunkered down. His jaw fell, and he slouched over backward so that he seated himself heavily.

"Holy cow!" he gulped.

The rescued man was not Ham.

Long Tom stared at the man. "Who the devil are you?"

The man was lean, rather thin about the waist, but muscled sufficiently. His clothing was expensive, perfectly tailored, and still remarkably neat, considering what he had been through. In these two respects, he resembled Ham, the dapper lawyer who was one of Doc Savage's five associates.

The man tried to answer—for he was not gagged. But the sounds he made were unintelligible. He seemed to be far gone.

"Get that string off his throat," Renny muttered. "Maybe he's choking."

They loosened the string. Then the man fell over and his face buried itself in a pool of rainwater. Breath came out of his lungs and made a loud bubbling.

"Fainted," Doc said, and lifted the man.

In the far distance, three reports smacked out rapidly. They sounded very much like shots.

Chapter 7

THE WHITE-BROWN MEN

The reports were shots discharged from one of the lean-barreled foreign automatics, and were directed at the front tire of a police motorcycle. The cars had been driving fast enough to interest the motorcycle cop.

The front tire of the motorcycle let go with a loud hissing. The cop fought the handlebars, but his machine wobbled into a ditch and bucked him off. He wallowed for a time in the water that filled the ditch, then got out and tried to use his revolver. But the cars bearing the brown men were too far distant.

The machines—there were two of them—speeded on for a short distance, then turned to the right and slowed down.

"He is a fool who only drops thorns in the path of the tiger," one brown man told the man who had fired at the motorcycle cop. "The tiger will come again by another route."

"He is a greater fool who kills the cub of the tiger," retorted the other. "The police of these white devil ghosts are a bad tiger."

Monk, who rode in the same car, his head encased in a gunnysack, growled, "If I ever get loose, I'm gonna make somebody think tiger!"

A man leaned forward, selected the spot in the sack where Monk's nose should be, and tapped with a hard brown fist. The homely chemist bawled out and tried to kick, using both of his feet, which were now bound together. There was some excitement while he was beaten to the point where he concluded it was the better course to submit to his captors.

By that time, the cars had stopped.

"It is a wise leopard who changes his spots," stated one of the captors.

They unloaded from the two machines. Men went carefully over the cars with handkerchiefs, rubbing vigorously to remove finger prints. Then they advanced on foot.

Ahead, there was a traffic light which still functioned, although the traffic was very light. The Orientals scattered themselves and became lost in the darkness, dragging their prisoners along with them.

A moment later a motorist, stopping for the red light, got quite a shock when brown men suddenly descended upon him from either side, menacing with their thin-barreled guns. The motorist, not being devoid of sense, put up his hands. He was hauled out, struck over the head repeatedly until he was thoroughly senseless, then tossed behind a near-by wooden fence.

Within the next ten minutes, a second motorist met an identical fate.

The brown men loaded into the cars thus obtained and drove off. Their pace was now decorous, so as not to cause a repetition of the motorcycle cop incident.

It rained again, more violently this time, so that water stood in a sheet over the streets and ran mad torrents in the gutters. Traffic policemen were grotesque black figures in their raincoats and cap shields.

Monk and Ham were kept out of sight, and by now were gagged so effectively that they could make no noise audible outside the cars. The brown Tananese were unusually silent.

They drove down, finally, on a steep road that led to the bank of the Hudson, below Riverside Drive. Monk and Ham were hauled out, their ankles untied; gun muzzles forced them to walk ahead. They came to a large, shadowy building, on which a man played a flashlight, disclosing a sign that read:

CLOSED
BY ORDER OF PARK COMMISSION

The building behind the sign was soundless, and the flash beam, roving, picked up a name painted over the door:

COASTAL YACHT CLUB

A brown Tananese called out softly; a voice answered from the door, and they all filed inside. Monk and Ham were now unhooded and ungagged.

Great red welts were to be seen across the hands and faces of the two prisoners. These stood out like streaks of scarlet grease paint, when bathed by the occasional dabbing touch of a roving flashlight beam.

The brown men arrayed themselves along one wall, opposite a blank wall, and turned out their lights. The darkness became like a black solid. They waited for a moment in silence. Then one spoke hollowly, dramatically, after the manner of one expecting something momentous.

"We wait your presence, O One Who Died Before Time Began," he said.

And the strange voice which Monk and Ham had heard earlier in the night near the water front, said, "My green soul is with you. It will take the visible form of a face."

Monk, hearing that, gave a violent start and rolled his eyes toward the source of the voice. Locating it, he started again and blinked incredulously.

Across the room, fully twenty feet distant, was a face, a grisly, luminous visage, its hue a bilious green. The lineaments were, weirdly enough, now scarcely suggestive of an Oriental countenance. The mouth opened and the tongue was like a pale, vague tendril of flame behind the uncannily glowing teeth. The whole effect was that of a luminous ghost.

The spokesman of the brown men got down on his knees and touched his forehead to the floor.

"The soul of this one is a worm which has been stepped upon," he said uneasily. "My words are vehicles which convey naught but bad news. For that, sorrow fills me."

Monk watched the fantastic green face. He strained his eyes until they hurt. Yet he could discern no form below the verdant countenance. It was as if the face were a thing disembodied, something unreal.

A spell had gripped the brown men of Tanan. They seemed hardly to breathe. And each had clasped both his fists and pressed them tightly to his forehead, holding them there. No doubt this latter was some gesture of submission peculiar to Tananese.

"My soul is a worm, my body quivers like the flank of the trapped mountain deer and my ancestors all hide their faces in shame, for I have failed to carry out the wishes of He Who Has Been Dead A Thousand Thousand Years, the Mystic Mullah," said the brown spokesman. "Here are the events that brought me shame as they happened——"

The recital was long-winded, but when it ended, the speaker had conveyed the story of what had happened at the abandoned refinery.

"We were dogs and fled," he finished. "And this bronze man, this white devil ghost who is not white, took from us our third prisoner. Truly, we are alley curs that we permitted this."

"You are dogs," the macabre voice of the Mystic Mullah agreed. "But you are wise dogs, like those that grow to a ripe old age in the alleys of Tanan, because they know when to run and when to fight."

"Such praise from you is beautiful," murmured the other. "It is like perfume in our nostrils, nectar in our mouths and wine in our bellies. What is your next wish?"

"The death of the bronze man," advised the Mystic Mullah.

No one appeared to have a ready answer to that. Several men breathed noisily. A knife fell out of one man's sleeve, making a ringing noise, and he snatched it up with the guilty expression of a small boy caught bringing candy into a school room.

Monk sat down on the floor, doing so slowly, as if he were tired. He ignored a harsh hiss from his captor commanding him to stand erect; and the captor, seemingly loath to create a stir in the presence of the hideous green countenance that was suspended apparently in thin air, crouched down beside Monk and thrust the point of a knife a quarter of an inch into Monk's back and held it there, an agonizing threat.

The Mystic Mullah continued speaking.

"This white devil ghost who is not white, this Doc Savage, must not have his ears filled with the tale borne by the woman, Joan Lyndell, and the milk-hearted camel who is the Khan Nadir Shar of Tanan," the hollow voice said. "So far, we have done well. The messenger, Hadim, died in trying to reach the bronze man. Then, making use of the actor fool who sold himself for a few dollars, we got Joan Lyndell and the Khan into our trap, which we sprung after some difficulty."

The spokesman of the brown men asked, "But what of the third prisoner, the one who was taken from us?"

"He is but a moth drawn to the flame," said the Mystic Mullah.

The mouthpiece of the group of brown men was puzzled.

"Your wisdom is too profound," he mumbled. "Will you speak in small words that your children may comprehend?"

"You may forget the third prisoner," advised the Mystic Mullah. "Worry not about him, and harm him not, for he has a use to us."

The other chuckled suddenly. "Your small words carry the light. This third prisoner, he is one of your servants."

"Seek not to comprehend that which is known only to the One Who Has Been Dead A Thousand Thousand Years," the Mystic Mullah suggested.

Monk squirmed to get away from the knife pricking his back. He could feel scarlet trickling down inside his undershirt. It felt like a string of flies crawling on his bare skin.

Monk growled—unintelligibly, so it sounded to his captors. The sounds Monk made were guttural, little more than audible. They might have been the mutterings of a man afraid to speak.

Actually, Monk's growled sounds were quite intelligible —to half a dozen men in the civilized world. The words were Mayan, tongue of the lost race which once populated Central America; and the language which Doc Savage and his five aides had learned, that they might communicate with each other without being understood by those about them.

Ham heard the words, and began shifting his position in an endeavor to get close to Monk. His legs were not bound; neither were those of the homely chemist.

"We know much of this bronze man," said the Mystic Mullah. "Through the eyes of you, my servants, we have studied his institution in this great city of the white devil ghosts. We know that he values the lives of the five men who aid him above all else. Of that knowledge, we shall make use, for we have two of his assistants with us."

Monk sighed loudly.

Ham promptly kicked the temple of the brown man who held the knife against Monk's back.

Ham wore shoes with narrow toes, and his kick was terrific. The knife-man upset, dragging his blade across Monk's back, slitting his clothing and raking across his bare flesh.

Monk squawled, "You could've done a better kickin' job than that, you danged shyster!" and shot to his feet like a toy spring snake coming out of a box. He continued straight for the fantastic face which was suspended in mid-air. Reaching it, he launched a terrific kick at where the body should be.

His foot whistled through empty space. Momentum spun him around. Off balance, he slammed down. In falling, though, he did not take his startled eyes from the unholy visage. Thus it was that he saw an impossible phenomenon.

The unearthly green glow that was the face seemed to fade, becoming paler and paler until its outlines were lost to the eyes and only a vague luminance remained. That, too, went away, leaving only the blackness of the room.

"Lights!" bawled a voice in Tananese.

Another man wailed, "He who shows a light in the presence of the Mystic Mullah is the same as a dying man———"

"Lights!" screamed the other. "Fool! The Mystic Mullah has become as the air we breath. Can you not see that? Lights!"

Some one knocked the lens out of a flashlight, so that it whitened the whole room palely when it was thumbed on.

Monk, peering about, was struck with a species of surprise paralysis, for the doors of the room were closed tightly, the windows boarded over from the outside so that there was hardly a crack. And nowhere was there a trace of the sinister presence, the Mystic Mullah. Nor was there anything to explain that nature of the eerie green visage which had been suspended in the darkness.

Brown men pitched upon Monk, and the homely chemist backed away. One man came close, holding a knife with both hands. Monk kicked. The knife wielder flopped away with most of his lower face out of shape. Across the room, Ham was also fighting, using only his feet.

"It is intended that their lives be tools of the Mystic Mullah!" rapped the spokesman. "Do not kill. He Who Has Been Dead A Thousand Thousand Years would not want his tools destroyed."

Ham promptly stopped struggling and barked at Monk, "Don't be a dope, you ape! They're not going to kill us!"

Monk snarled, "Swell!" and jumped up amazingly and kicked a wiry brown chest with both feet. Ribs broke in the chest with a sound distinctly audible. Then a Tananese ran around behind the gorilla of a chemist and banged him twice over the head with a long-barreled automatic. Monk sat down with a cloud in his eyes.

Both Monk and Ham were now bound more securely. The gags were replaced. Then one of the brown men went outside, to return with the word that all was quiet.

"This is a remote spot," he reported. "We are as alone as the wolf which howls in the desert."

Then he started violently and looked at his own hands. From them, he shifted his stare to his fellows.

"Look!" he gulped.

They all looked. Strange expressions came upon their faces, expressions of bewilderment admixed with fear. Again and again, they examined their hands or peered at each other's faces. They rubbed their hands together violently, as if washing them. They produced handkerchiefs and scrubbed; then shook heads slowly.

Their hands, their faces, were slowly turning white. Or perhaps the color was more of a gray, the tint that comes over a corpse after death. The effect upon the brown skins was hideous.

"We are dying, and yet we live!" a man groaned.

Several planted clasped fists against their foreheads and began to call loudly upon their ancestors. Their voices trembled with the fright that the onrush of gray color was bringing. It was the spokesman, obviously the most alert-minded of the lot, who spoke up loudly.

"Offspring of donkeys!" he growled. "This is the hand of the Mystic Mullah, whose powers no man can comprehend. He has seen fit to give us the skins of the white devil ghosts, that we may better serve him without attracting attention."

"Truly the ways of Him Who Has Existed A Thousand Thousand Years are marvelous," murmured another, relieved.

Monk stared at them. His little eyes were bright in their pits of gristle. He looked at his own hands. They, too, were assuming an unholy gray tint.

Monk made a noisy laughing sound through his nose.

Chapter 8

THE WISE GUY

William Harper Littlejohn spun his monocle so that its black ribbon wrapped around his finger, bandage fashion, then unwound it with a backward movement. His finger seemed but a linkage of bone with a thin skin painted on.

"Indicative omens point to the reanimation of the individual shortly," he said.

"Hurrah!" Renny said gloomily. "Those are the smallest words you have used in the last half hour."

Long Tom, who was guiding their car through the fog and the rain, only frowned and rubbed a faint fog off the inside of the windshield with a palm.

Doc Savage was working over the lean, thin-waisted man whom they had rescued from the brown-skinned fiends of Tanan. His exploring fingers had located numerous head bruises which might have come from clubbing guns. It must have been the compounded effect of these, coupled with the excitement of the rescue, which had caused the man to pass out.

Doc had been administering restoratives for some time, but the man was only now showing signs of returning consciousness. He stirred, a little animation came into his fingers and his mouth fell open. Then his eyelids came apart.

"He is not human," he said.

His words were distinct. He had a nice voice.

"Not human," he mumbled again.

Johnny, Renny and Long Tom exchanged glances. Doc's features remained inscrutable.

"Who you talkin' about?" Renny rumbled.

The thin-waisted man squirmed about and finally managed to prop himself erect by using his arms as rigid stilts. He shut his eyes with great force several times, opening them wide after each pinching effort.

"*Whew!*" he muttered. "My head!"

Renny got down in front of him, his long face violent above an outthrust jaw, and growled, "Who were you mumblin' about when you woke up?"

"The Mystic Mullah," said the other distinctly. "Who the deuce are you?"

Then he rolled his eyes again, swiped his lips with his tongue and, quite suddenly, lay back in the car seat.

"Halleluiah!" he said dryly. "We are saved!"

Long Tom took his eyes off the road long enough to say, "Sounds like he's nuts."

Doc Savage watched the thin-waisted man closely and asked, "What day of the week is this?"

"Wednesday," said the other man. "Granting of course that it is now past midnight. Haven't you more sensible questions?"

"His head is clear enough," Doc said. "What is your name?"

"It might be Mohammed, or Little Boy Blue, or Columbus," said the stranger. "But, of course, it's not."

Renny blocked out a big fist, held it close to the man's head, and head and fist did not differ greatly in size.

The stranger looked at the knuckles almost against his nose, let his jaw down in mock wonder, and asked, "What on earth is that?"

"That's what cracks wise-crackers," Renny told him. "Now are you gonna talk sense or do I have to start the bells ringing in your head?"

"Push the button," said the other. "Or go straight to the devil. Take your choice."

Long Tom turned his head to ask, "What's eating him? Is he really ga-ga?"

Doc Savage said, "It seems that the gentleman does not want to talk."

They drove on rapidly, down in the business section now, but well out of the theatrical district where cars were few and only an occasional trolley banged along, or an elevated train made greater uproar. The fog was a gray-black packing in the street, and everything was shiny and wet, with water running in the gutters or streaming off eaves. It seemed as if the entire world were turning to wetness.

The thin-waisted man looked out of the moving car and said, "Noah must have had a night like this."

Renny roared, "Guy, are you gonna talk?"

The stranger laughed shrilly, then shut his eyes as if it had hurt him.

"Gentlemen, are you obtuse?" he asked. "No, I am not talking. I thought I had made that clear."

Johnny carefully wrapped his magnifying monocle in a

handkerchief and tucked it in his upper coat pocket, a precaution he habitually took when there was danger of it getting broken. Then he began searching the stranger, obviously prepared for resistance. But the well-dressed man did not show fight.

"As the Mystic Mullah's faithful say: 'He is a wise man who knows when to do nothing'," he murmured.

Johnny turned the fellow's pockets inside out. He looked in his clothing for labels. The total result was a blank.

"I was gone over thoroughly earlier in the night and relieved of all my possessions," said the man.

"This individual is the personification of ambiguity," Johnny stated.

"Does a dictionary go with that?" asked the man.

Long Tom wheeled the sedan up by the side of the towering skyscraper which housed Doc's headquarters. He touched a button under the dash; this actuated the searchlight projecting infra-red light with which all of his cars were fitted, and the invisible beam in turn reacted upon a photo-electric cell connected to an electromagnet that released the lock of the garage door.

Long Tom drove in and down the ramp, the door closing automatically behind him. The opening mechanism was convenient, because the sedan was bulletproofed, and no one need leave its shelter to open the doors.

"What about your roadster?" Renny asked the bronze man.

Doc had left the roadster back on the lane near the abandoned refinery. He had rode into town with the others in order that he might question the stranger they had rescued.

"It will be all right where it is until we have time to go after it," Doc said.

The stranger was looking about curiously, but he said nothing. They entered an elevator at the end of a passage. The cage was of unusually stout construction.

Doc threw the control and the cage accelerated at tremendous speed. The stranger, taken by surprise, was snapped down flat on the floor; but the others, knowing the pace of the elevator, kept their feet.

The stranger got up, looking sheepish, then instinctively grabbed a hand rail as the cage stopped so swiftly that it seemed they were suspended in mid-air.

"This is better than an amusement park ride," he said shakily.

"Pipe down," Renny advised him. "You're getting in my hair!"

"Wait!" Doc Savage advised, as Long Tom was about to open the elevator door.

The bronze man pointed at a small perforation in the sliding doors. Through this, it was possible to view a stationary mirror fixed to the door frame. This gave a view of the corridor.

"Holy cow!" Renny thumped.

There was a policeman lounging in front of Doc Savage's office.

With no further hesitation, Doc opened the elevator doors and stepped into the corridor, the rest of the party behind him.

The policeman, recognizing Doc, stepped up to him and said, "Mr. Savage, the commissioner sent me up here to see what you know about the Oriental found dead with a broken neck in this corridor." The copper was a bit overawed in Doc's presence, for he shifted nervously on his feet.

"Tell the commissioner," Doc said, "that, as yet, the entire case is a mystery to me; but that as soon as I get to the heart of the plot, I will notify him."

"O. K., Mr. Savage." The policeman saluted snappily and made for the elevator.

Doc entered his office.

Then they all stepped into the great laboratory with its fabulous array of scientific apparatus, its thousands of bottles of chemicals, its maze of electrical wiring.

The thin-waisted stranger glanced about with manifest interest.

"Quite effective," he drawled.

Renny ran huge fingers through his hair.

"We've got to find Monk and Ham, somehow," he rumbled. "And if we don't get going pretty soon, it'll make things harder."

"We've got to find Joan Lyndell and the Khan Nadir Shar," added Long Tom.

"I thought so," said the stranger.

Renny scowled at him. "You thought what?"

"What a sad face you have, grandma," murmured the stranger.

"You are a hegemonic enigma," the gaunt Johnny told him.

"You," said the stranger, "stun me with those words."

Long Tom, the electrical wizard, snapped, "We're killing time, blast it! How are we going to get a line on Monk and Ham?"

As if to explain that, Doc Savage went to the telephone,

took down the receiver and began to speak. The mouthpiece was fitted with a boxlike attachment which partially enclosed the face and made his words inaudible to those in the room. He spoke for some time. Then he hung up.

Long Tom was staring at the bronze man's hands.

"Doc!" he exploded. "Look at your hands! Your face! The skin is turning white!"

It was dawn. The fog had gone away, pushed by a cold wind from the north, and the morning sun was incredibly bright. Only the uncommon cleanness of the streets showed how wet the night had been.

Long Tom had gone downstairs to get the morning newspapers. He returned now. Ordinarily, he looked unhealthy, but now he was starkly white of skin, as bleached as if his hide had turned to typewriter paper.

Doc Savage, Renny, Johnny, even the stranger—who had still not talked—were also weirdly white. There had been discussion during the final hours of the night concerning this strange pallor.

But Doc Savage had taken no part in the talk, had seemed unconcerned, and the others, noting this, had not worried excessively. If the whiteness had been dangerous, Doc would have taken action upon it, they reasoned.

Long Tom deposited his bundle of papers.

"Nothing new in them," he advised.

"Did you look at the advertisements?" Doc asked.

"Why should I?" the electrical wizard countered.

Doc Savage riffled through the papers. One after the other, he spread them open on a table displaying in each instance a full-page advertisement.

"The results of my telephone call," he said.

"Holy cow!" Renny boomed when he saw the displays.

The advertisements were in bold black type. Each was worded the same, reading:

$1,000 REWARD FOR GHOST MAN

The sum of one thousand dollars will be paid for information leading to the whereabouts of a man whose skin is unnaturally white. This man will have the face of an Oriental. His skin will be almost as white as ordinary writing paper.

Call this newspaper when you see such a man.

"Holy cow!" Renny repeated wonderingly. Then he eyed

Doc Savage. "So this white skin is your doing! How'd you work it?"

"A chemical vapor," Doc explained. "It is odorless and colorless at first, but upon long exposure to the oxygen in the air, it turns white. It is harmless."

"But where did you use it?" Renny persisted.

"At the refinery," Doc told him. "The stuff was in two cans thrown in such a position that the Mystic Mullah's men had to walk through them."

Long Tom said grimly, "But they'll get wise! All they have to do is dye their skins, or cover them with grease paint."

"It will not be effective," Doc told him. "This chemical stains material with which it comes in contact. For instance, examine your clothing."

Long Tom scrutinized his coat sleeve closely, and it dawned on him that the cloth was several shades lighter than it had been originally.

"So all we have to do is wait for some one to sight one of these white-skinned brown men," he grinned.

"The newspapers have orders to relay any reports to us," Doc said.

The stranger had taken it all in.

"Have you any more hats with rabbits in them?" he queried dryly.

Renny scowled. "How about me bumping this guy around a little, Doc?"

The telephone rang. It was one of the newspaper offices.

"A man with a white skin was sighted a few minutes ago," said the informant at the news plant.

"The address, please," Doc requested.

The other rattled off an address.

"Sorry," Doc told him. "That man was not an Oriental."

He hung up.

"Who did they see?" Long Tom demanded.

"You," Doc told him. "Some one must have seen you when you were down buying the newspapers."

The phone rang again. The bronze man—he was not bronze now, due to the whitening effect of the chemical—answered and listened. He hung up.

"Man out for a morning walk along the Hudson River saw an Oriental with a white skin enter one of the yacht clubs which the city park commissioner ordered abandoned some weeks ago," Doc said.

Renny said grimly, "Let's go!"

Half an hour later, Doc Savage was saying, "Johnny, you

and Long Tom cover the river. These fellows are smart enough to overlook no bets. They may have a get-away by water arranged."

"Supermalagorgeous!" Johnny agreed.

"Does the man know any small words?" queried the thin-waisted stranger sarcastically.

Renny said, "Shut up, pal, or I'll bust your face in!"

Johnny and Long Tom shoved off. They were in a speedboat, a lean, heavy craft which carried so much engine that it seemed on the point of sinking whenever it was not in motion. The propellers threw a great geyser of spray, but there was little noise except for their churn, the engines being excellently muffled. Within a hundred yards, the craft was doing forty knots.

Johnny and Long Tom had gotten the speedboat from a seaplane hangar and boathouse owned by Doc Savage, which masqueraded as a disused warehouse on the Hudson River water front.

Doc Savage now led the way to his car, Renny following with the stranger. This was a different machine, but armor-plated like the others. It, however, bore a license which had been issued to Doc under an assumed name. The machine got into motion quietly.

Renny jabbed the waspish stranger with a thumb and asked, "What about Wise Snappers, here?"

Doc studied the man. "By not talking, you are making things difficult," he said.

"What a beautiful speech," smirked the other.

"That's the last straw," rumbled Renny, and swung a fist. The huge maul of bone and gristle seemed certain to hit the mysterious man, to batter him into insensibility. But it did not.

The slender man rolled his head, boxer fashion. The blow went harmlessly past. Then he hit Renny a terrific, blinding blow on the jaw.

They both looked surprised; Renny because he had been hit so unexpectedly, the stranger because he expected Renny to go down and nothing of the sort had happened. The next instant, there was violent turmoil in the rear of the sedan. Terrific blows smacked. The two men grunted. Both, it was plain, were skilled boxers, but there was little room for that in the car.

Renny, by the simple process of using his superior weight to force the other down on the floorboards, got him helpless, then clipped him into senselessness with a big fist.

"That guy can fight," Renny said grimly. "But what gets

me is the way he's acting. Notice he hasn't made any effort to get away from us. He never even asked what we intended to do to him."

"Strange," Doc agreed.

"What are we gonna do with him?" Renny wanted to know.

For answer, Doc Savage produced a small hypodermic from a pocket of the car.

"I brought this for his benefit," he said. "It will keep him unconscious until a stimulant and counteractive are administered."

Renny took the hypodermic needle, leaned over and used it on the unconscious stranger. The man—he was stirring a little with returning consciousness—relaxed and began to breathe more easily and noisily.

"Now, how are we gonna get into that yacht club?" Renny asked. "We can't just barge in."

"That," Doc told him, "is exactly what we are going to do—barge up."

Chapter 9

TROUBLE CLUB

The Coastal Yacht Club was one of the oldest and most distinguished in the United States, and it had occupied its site on the banks of the Hudson River since Colonial days. But the last city administration had taken over the shore line along the stretch by the club with the intention of establishing a park. There had been a squabble in the courts, after which the yacht club abandoned its large but ancient building and betook its membership further uptown.

The old club lay now, awaiting the wreckers, a forlorn, rambling white structure of wood extending partially over the river, and with a flagpole which was a little off plumb.

It was shortly after eight o'clock when a puffing tug escorted a large empty barge to the ramshackle yacht club dock. At the dock, moored stem and stern so that its paintwork would not be chafed, lay a small cabin cruiser. There was no one aboard.

The barge was nursed up to the dock and lines made fast, then the tug skipper cast off and chugged away down the river. The two bargemen scrambled ashore.

They were very grimy specimens, these two, wearing old clothing too voluminous even for the chilly morning, and oilskin southwesters which made it seem as if they had been out all night in the fog and rain.

Heads down, they shuffled to the club, seeming in no hurry as they reached the porch and seated themselves. One kept his hands out of sight a great deal.

"Thought that wreckin' crew was supposed to be here by this time," he said loudly at last.

"Let's get our tools ashore," growled the other.

They left the porch, went to the barge and returned bearing large, grimy canvas sacks. They deposited one of these on the wharf, another on the rear porch of the yacht club, and went around to the front and placed another on the porch there. Then they seated themselves and resumed talking.

"Strange the wreckers ain't showed up," said the one who kept his hands out of sight.

"Yeah," agreed the other. "Let's look inside and see how much of a job this is gonna be."

They both got up and ambled to the door. They tried to peer inside, but dust had settled on the glass panel, shutting out vision. They tried to open the door, but it resisted their efforts. One of them pulled out a key and started to insert it in the lock.

The door opened suddenly. With great speed, the two shabby wreckers sprang forward. They might have been expecting this.

Inside the yacht club, a man squawked in surprise. He was an Oriental who had once been brown of skin, but who was now a weirdly bleached fellow. The man had held a knife; but the door, slamming into him, had taken the knife point and he was wrenching to get it free.

A fist banged the man's head and he fell down heavily, leaving the knife sticking in the door. The fist was a tremendous thing, and it belonged to the wrecker who had been keeping his hands out of sight.

There were two more knife wielders inside the door.

The two wreckers had changed character remarkably. No one could mistake their identity now. They were Doc Savage and Renny.

The two knifemen—white-brown men—saw they had caught Tartars; but they had nerve and did not try to retreat, endeavoring to get in with ripping knife strokes. Their skill was evident as they lunged.

Both saw their knife strokes were going home to the chests of their foes. Doc and Renny seemed strangely clumsy, defenseless. Knife point traveling at blinding speed, one of the knives hit Doc almost in the pit of the stomach. But instead of penetrating, there was a rasp of a noise and the blade broke off short.

A blow clanked on the knife wielder's head and he fell. Probably he had not even had time to realize Doc was wearing a bulletproof vest.

The other knifeman made an industrious effort to sink his blade into Renny, discovered the bulletproof vest too late, and was slammed down.

Shrill Tananese squawls were piping through the ancient building. They conveyed wild alarm.

Doc and Renny charged forward. Their procedure might have seemed reckless, but not only did they wear the armor vests which protected their bodies, legs, and even a portion of their necks, but the oilskin hats which they wore were not conventional seamen's hats at all, but thin steel helmets as efficient as regulation army equipment.

A labyrinth of passages and stairs opened ahead of them. Boarded-up windows made the interior murky, almost dark, in spite of the morning brilliance outside. In the gloom, white-brown men flitted like ghosts. Occasional shots whooped.

"Monk!" Renny boomed. "Ham! You in here?"

In answer to that, a scuffle started somewhere in the rear.

"That'll be them!" Renny growled.

The big-fisted engineer and the bronze man dived in that direction. They made ghostly figures with their unnaturally white skins, their grim expressions.

A cluster of animated men appeared ahead, vague figures in the gloom. Monk and Ham were putting up a fight, hoping to prevent themselves being carried away. Able to use only their bound legs and arms, they were not doing badly.

Gun flame lashed out, and the room filled with ear-splitting concussion as guns were discharged. The spike-snouted automatics had a particularly vicious crack, and the bullets, driven with force enough to penetrate anything less than extraordinarily efficient bulletproof vests, delivered tremendous blows.

Doc and Renny separated, getting down behind large steel cabinets. This had evidently been the club locker room, and the lockers had not yet been removed. The Tananese, disgusted and excited, drove a few bullets through metal cabinets. They cackled orders among themselves.

Renny had expected them to charge. He was surprised when they did not.

"What're they up to?" he demanded loudly.

"They're trying to take the prisoners away," Doc called.

A door banged in the extreme rear; then the room became quiet. Doc and Renny reared up simultaneously, charged the panel and found it barred on the inside. Renny put his huge fists to use, smashing with a violence that seemed incredible. He pulled splinter-edged slabs out of the door, got the panel open, and he and Doc whipped through.

Steps slanted downward.

"Back stairs!" Renny roared.

"Wait!" Doc rapped. "Listen!"

They listened, and they could hear running feet in the halls below, heard doors bang open, and caught the weaker pipe of Oriental voices outside.

"They're out!" Renny growled.

Doc Savage jerked his coat back, wrenched and got the

skirt of his bulletproof tunic up. This disclosed a small case which had been well protected. Projecting from the case was a knob resembling those on radio sets, and a pointer was affixed to this. In a circle around the pointer, four numerals were stamped. Where the pointer now rested, the panel was marked "Off."

Doc turned the pointer to the first number.

Outside, there was a loud, mushy explosion, as if some one had dropped a rotten egg several feet in diameter.

The bleached brown men began to scream and cackle like guineas.

"Hah!" roared Renny. "I guess they didn't expect that!"

Doc Savage said nothing, but turned the knob to the next number. This resulted in another explosion. The first had been at the rear, but the second occurred around in front. A fresh caterwauling of sound arose from the Orientals.

"Now's our chance," said Renny, needlessly, for Doc Savage was already racing downstairs.

They plunged out of the yacht club building, and were suddenly among a forest of squirming, yelling men. The bleached brown fellows—those immediately at the door—were not showing fight. They were interested solely in their own difficulties, in the thing which had happened to them.

They looked as if they had been pierced by thousands of needles, or perhaps caught in a storm of fine, flying shot. Drops of scarlet, very tiny, were oozing from their skins in such profusion that the result was a freckled appearance.

Odor of burned powder hung in the air. A small cloud of powder smoke made a haze over the mêlée. Scattered about were the fragments of the tool bag which Doc Savage had placed on the yacht club porch.

The Tananese began toppling over, contorted, mouths gaping.

Renny snorted gleefully and waded through them. Doc's tool bags had been bombs, exploded by remote radio control. They had been filled, not with deadly shrapnel, but with solidified particles of the same chemical which the dapper Ham employed to coat the tip of his sword cane. The stuff looked like a yellowish rock salt.

"Holy cow!" Renny boomed. "Monk and Ham are not here!"

That was true. Neither the homely chemist nor the lawyer was in sight.

Foot clatter came from the direction of the dock. View of

the structure was impeded by a boat shed. Doc whipped around that—and almost fell over two prone figures, both of which were bound and gagged.

They were the girl, Joan Lyndell, and the hawk-nosed Khan Nadir Shar. The pair rolled their eyes imploringly at the bronze man.

On ahead, out toward the dock end, fully a dozen of the Tananese were racing for the moored cabin cruiser. Among them, they carried two limp figures which were bundled in old canvas, probably abandoned sails which they had picked up around the yacht club. Little about the shrouded forms could be distinguished.

Among the Tananese was one who kept his head covered. He was a towering, gaunt figure, stooped in an effort to hide some of his height. And he had pulled his coat up over his head so that it was covered. He ran in the lead, as if more anxious than the others to escape.

On the ground in front of Doc, the Khan Nadir Shar wrenched about. He got his hands up. His fingers had been stripped of jewels, but grooves where the rings had rested were distinguishable. He managed to get the gag out.

"Your men, Monk and Ham, they carry them away!" he rapped in English which was still unnaturally perfect in spite of its staccato speed. "And seize the one who has his head hidden with a coat!"

Doc ran toward the wharf end.

The Tananese pitched the two shrouded forms which they carried, and the figures landed on the trunk of the cabin cruiser. Brown men leaped down and whisked them inside. One seized the controls. A starter gnashed at a flywheel with iron teeth. The motor banged into life.

All but two Tananese were now aboard. These two took a great leap to the top of the cockpit cover. This broke, letting them through on the man who still had his coat over his head. He fell down, but did not uncover his head, then got up and kicked soundly in the ribs the two who had broken through.

The cabin cruiser was moving now. Its propeller threw a plume of water. The pilot put the wheel hard over.

"Damn!" Renny roared, and looked as if he were going to plunge in after the craft.

Doc Savage hauled him back—then gave him a violent shove. Renny flailed his arms, turned over once and made a great splash. Doc hit the water almost simultaneously.

Renny came up, spouted and started to yell.

"Down!" Doc rapped. "Stay under!"

There was a loud *chung!* as a bullet hit water. Others followed. Lead-knocked spray stung Renny's eyes. The Tananese were leaning over the cabin cruiser cockpit, shooting with the wildness characteristic of excited Orientals.

Renny bloated his lungs with air and sank. He knew now why Doc had shoved him overboard then dived in himself. On the flimsy dock they would have stood no chance. Finding a dock spile, Renny hugged it and remained down until his lungs took fire and his ears began to bang in sympathy with his heartbeat.

He came up half expecting to find the cabin cruiser had come back. But it was not there. Far down the river, it scudded like a fat white duck.

The explanation of its continued flight was moaning out on the river: the speedboat occupied by Johnny and Long Tom. The speedboat had been loitering slowly, its stern sunk far down. But now it was up on the surface so high that it seemed only propellers and rudder were buried in water.

In toward the dock boiled the speedboat. It cut its speed, settled, then seemed to stand on its stern as Johnny slammed the reverse lever.

Doc Savage stroked to the craft and whipped over the gunwale. Renny splashed up. Long Tom seized both of his big wrists. The two of them were nearly yanked overboard as Johnny snapped the throttle around on the quadrant. Renny finally landed on the floorboards, sputtering, clothes leaking water. When he got up again, the speed of the boat was such that the rush of air almost knocked him over.

Johnny cut the exhaust streams from the mufflers. Quiet was no longer necessary; and the cutting out of the silencers added a little to the boat's power. The water was rough; the hull smacked down on the waves with a series of loud reports.

Other clapping sounds began to be heard. The non-shatter windshield acquired round perforations; streaks of splinters arose on the mahogany coaming.

"They sure do like us," Long Tom said grimly. "I hope they haven't anything stronger than those foreign pistols."

"A propensity conducive to salubriousness," agreed Johnny. He had jacked a periscope up and was using it to steer by.

Bullets fired from the cabin cruiser continued to nick the speedboat hull, but did no harm, because the craft had been conceived and designed for a violent existence. It was armored as heavily as circumstances permitted; under the innocent-looking mahogany sheeting was a layer of nickel-chrome alloy, carbonized and tempered like the plate on battleships.

Doc opened a locker, got out another periscope and employed it to watch the cabin crusier. The craft was swinging out across the river, bound north.

"Heading for the Jersey shore," he advised.

Renny, who was never too cautious, popped up his head for a brief look.

"They'll make it, too," he rumbled. "Got a head start on us when Johnny swung in to pick us up."

For a moment there was only the terrific bawl of the motors and the loud reports of waves smacking past.

"They've got Monk and Ham wrapped in sailcloth!" Renny boomed. "Blast it! I hope they're still alive!"

Doc said nothing. He was watching the cabin cruiser. It was headed for a stretch of beach, one of the few along the river.

Beyond the beach, clinging to the steep slope of the bank, was an amusement park. This was closed for the winter. It had a drear, deserted aspect.

The cabin cruiser scarcely slackened speed when it came to the beach. Propellers and rudder were torn off. The craft slid twice its own length out of water.

The Tananese picked themselves up and began to spill out. First to hit the ground was the tall man who kept his coat over his head.

The next men to spring out carried the two forms wrapped in sailcloth.

Johnny held the speedboat directly for the beach. Doc reached his side, said a word and Johnny surrendered the controls. Then Johnny, Long Tom and Renny draped themselves forward over the bullet-ripped coaming. They gripped cleats and wrenched them up, thus lifting special steel shields already fitted with slit loopholes. They leveled their mercy-bullet-charged supermachine pistols through these. The guns began to racket, and spew smoking empties.

The Tananese stood for a moment, trying to make a fight of it. Two went down. The tall man who kept his head covered, waved an arm and probably shouted orders which did not reach the speedboat. His party raced in wild retreat.

Doc jacked the speedboat engines into reverse. Some thousands of horsepower whooped and moaned. Mechanism strained. The braking shock sent all three men skidding off the coaming. Then the boat grounded lightly.

Doc took a running leap along the deck and reached dry land. His three men splashed out behind him. They ran furiously, using the machine pistols.

They shot freely, taking few pains to avoid hitting the two canvas-swathed forms. The mercy bullets would not harm Ham and Monk seriously, except on the rare chance of contact with an eye.

The Tananese reached a row of concession booths, all deserted and boarded up. Scrap trash and paper were scattered about. Gaudy paint had already started peeling from the booths and the amusement houses. The great framework of a roller-coaster had the aspect of a many-boned skeleton.

Dodging among the booths, the Tananese paused to shoot occasionally. They were fighting a difficult battle, and knew it by now. Doc and his men, with their effective body armor, were invulnerable to everything but a carefully placed shot.

Flight was not going to be easy, either, and the bleached brown men began to realize that, too. They took shelter among the buildings, found rests for their gun arms and started shooting with a great deal more accuracy.

Renny barked a pained surprise as a bullet made a rather gory mess of his left ear.

"Get down!" Doc directed. "Stay here!"

Renny boomed, "But Doc, if we circle around and cut 'em off, we'll be able——"

"Stay here!" the bronze man directed.

He crawled away, keeping below an ornamental sidewalk, and vanished behind a building which had a paint-scabby sign reading, "House of Mirrors." Renny, Long Tom and Johnny did not catch sight of him again.

Chapter 10

TWO MEN IN CANVAS

Renny clipped a fresh drum of mercy bullets into his machine pistol. The cartridges, waterproofed, had not suffered from the immersion.

The men lay behind a raised section of earth enclosed in a concrete retaining wall. This was less than a foot high, and had evidently supported one of the strength-testing devices in which a weight flies up a pole when a lever is struck with a mallet.

Several bullets sizzled overhead. Dirt, moist from the rain of the night before, showered them. It was chilly enough that their breath made faint steam. These spurts of steam came with surprising regularity considering the tenseness of the situation.

Renny looked repeatedly for Doc, but saw no sign of the bronze man.

"Doc must be gonna circle around behind," he decided.

"More likely he'll try to free Monk and Ham so those birds won't kill 'em," advised Long Tom.

"I hope Doc can grab the fellow who keeps his head covered," said Johnny. "It is my guess that that gentleman is the Mystic Mullah."

Both Renny and Long Tom glanced at the gaunt geologist. Johnny had not used words as small as those for some time. But Johnny had a habit of stepping out of the dictionary when the going got exceptionally rough.

"Look!" Renny exploded suddenly. He slanted a beam of an arm.

Several of the Tananese were scuttling across an open space. They dragged the two canvas-wrapped forms with them. They employed frenzied haste and kept low; then all dived into a huge circular building.

"What're we gonna do about this?" Renny growled. "Doc went around the other way."

"We were to stay here," Long Tom said grimly. "But that's Monk and Ham." He hurriedly snapped fresh ammo into his gun.

Johnny said, "Let's go!" and reared up.

They dashed to the left. A swarthy Tananese—he was one who had not been caught in the bleaching gas at the refinery, for his skin was still dark—fired at them. A blast from Long Tom's machine pistol drove him to cover.

Renny reached the side of the circular building. Johnny and Long Tom trod his heels. They could see the sign on the structure now. It read:

THE PHEHISTORIC WORLD

Running swiftly, Renny reached a side door. It was fastened with hasp and padlock, both rather flimsy. The big-fisted engineer holstered his machine pistol, grasped the padlock with both hands and wrenched and twisted. His great hands were corded blocks, his arms beams on which tendons stood out like rifle barrels. With a grinding and rasping of splinters, the staple came out.

They shoved through the door. There was a metal shield inside, no doubt intended to prevent non-paying customers seeing beyond the door. They rounded that.

"Holy cow!" Renny gulped, and dodged wildly.

It was very dark inside the great building, but a little light reflected through the door they had opened. This showed, close at hand, an astounding sight.

A fantastic monster was reared up on its hind legs. The thing was all of twenty feet high. It had giant rear legs, a hideous body covered with scales the size of pie plates, a head with predominantly gaping jaws and enormous fangs, to which clung drops of blood imitated realistically in red wax. The short front arms of the monster were out in front of the fangs, gripping what at first appeared to be the mutilated body of a hairy, apelike man.

"*Whew!*" Renny shuddered. "I thought at first that the body was Monk!"

The monster was one of the exhibits of the show, and the man-figure in its claws, a thing of papier-mâché and wax, was no doubt intended to represent a prehistoric man. There were other of the prehistoric Titans about. There was a long-necked brontosaurus, an amazing leer on its serpent face; there was another tyrannosaurus, such as held the likeness of the prehistoric man; there were various other dinosaurs; and suspended from the ceiling in lifelike immobility were various flying pterodactyls.

These latter, great hairless bats of things, were attached

to wires and aërial tracks; when the exhibit was in operation, they probably swooped about in a fashion calculated to make the hair of onlookers stand on end.

Near the front of the building, men could be heard moving about. There was a loud rustling. That meant some one had disturbed the artificial foliage which was a part of the display.

"Come on," Renny breathed, getting his great voice down to a whisper with some difficulty.

They advanced. It was difficult to keep from making noise in the artificial jungle. Not that the brown men were unaware that they were inside; the ripping off of the padlock had told them that. But it was just as well that they did not know from which direction the attack would come.

The jungle was surprisingly natural, and utterly fantastic, being composed of ferns the size of trees, and grasses which had blades fully fifteen feet high. All of this had been manufactured at some expense, and painted a natural green.

"Some joint!" Long Tom whispered.

"*Ps-s-t!*" Johnny admonished.

They listened until their ears hurt.

"What was it?" Long Tom breathed to Johnny.

Johnny replied, "I thought I heard something behind——"

Renny shrieked. They knew it was Renny, for there was no other voice quite like the roaring tones of the big-fisted engineer. The howl held on infinite agony.

Then Johnny felt a searing pain against one cheek. It was such a pain as he had never felt before. Reflex muscular action, instinctive movement, caused him to pitch sidewise. He crashed into a clump of prehistoric, reedlike grass. With a great crashing, he went down.

He felt the burning agony again. It was around one of his ankles this time. It crawled up his leg as far as his knee and grew and grew until the agony was almost insufferable. He bent over and struck furiously. His fingers began to burn. It was as if something terribly hot had taken hold of him.

Twisting about, Johnny managed to claw out matches. He could hear both Long Tom and Renny groaning and threshing about. He got his match aflame. His eyes popped.

There was a hideous green snakelike thing coiled over his ankles. Another floated in the air close to his hands. Even as he stared, it came toward his hands, seemed to wrap around them, and again he felt the frightful pain.

Johnny struck madly. The nebulous green thing was knocked away. But it came drifting back. He smashed at it once more—and missed. The green horror came on, touched his face, his nostrils.

The awful agony of it made Johnny yell until all of the air was gone out of his lungs; and then, when he sucked in breath again, the fearsome thing of green seemed to seize its chance and pounce into his mouth. Johnny coughed and gagged, fell back beating the air with his fists, writhing and twisting, and his heels beat at the floor with a mad frenzy.

After a while, he was still.

Long Tom and Renny also became quiet.

Doc Savage was some distance away when he heard the cries of his three men. The sounds were muffled, and because a street car was slamming past somewhere outside the park, he all but missed hearing the yells.

A weird phantom, the metallic giant whipped across the amusement park. His skin, thanks to the chemical bleaching fog, looked more like aluminum than bronze.

Tananese fired at him with pistols. There were two of them, and they shot madly, so that the hail of vicious lead drove Doc to the side, behind a boarded-up merry-go-round. He was delayed there some minutes until the two firing natives unaccountably deserted their posts and ran away across the amusement park grounds.

Doc went forward. He had some difficulty locating the source of the cries he had heard. There was only silence in the park now.

Not until he glimpsed the lock torn off the door of the circular building did he conclude the cries might have emanated from inside. He went to the door, listened. There was only silence.

He backed a pace, continued to listen. An utter calm had settled everywhere. Then, up the hill toward the gate, there was a stifled cry, an outburst of cackling Tananese.

Doc ran for the spot. His speed was tremendous. But long before he reached the gate he heard other cries, awful screams of one or two men in agony.

After that, an automobile motor roared, then receded; the violence of its noise indicating high speed.

Doc reached the gate.

Three men lay there. One wore shabby civilian garb, and on the front of his denim jumper clung a badge which said, "Watchman."

The other two were Jersey policemen in full uniform.

Two of them patently were dead, their heads twisted back in a grotesque manner which indicated broken necks. The third man still groveled about on the muddy ground, flailing and striking with both hands about his head, as if fighting something invisible. His neck bent by jerks, then straightened, only to bend again, as if something were trying to break it. His eyes were wide and glassy, but as he saw Doc Savage he tried to speak.

"Watchman heard shooting—called us," he gasped jerkily. "We came—green snakes in the air—men all got away in our car——"

Cluck! His head flew back, then forward, and hung like a ball on a string. An awful trembling went through his body and ran out to the ends of his arms, his legs, and he fell down heavily.

Doc Savage reached his side, making a furious endeavor to aid the man. But it was no use. The fellow's neck was broken.

Only for a few moments did Doc Savage stand studying the three dead men. The *cluck* he had heard had been the last victim's neck breaking. They all had broken necks. And there was no mark on their bodies, nothing that showed outwardly what had caused the grisly demise.

There were houses some distance down the road. Doc Savage ran to one of these, barged in on a frightened housewife and employed the telephone. He called the local police station, gave the shield numbers of the two dead officers and explained that they had been murdered, their car taken by the killers. Doc did not give his name, not wishing to be hampered by questions and by future police investigations. After the call, he went back to the amusement park.

Past the three dead men, he strode, only to turn back and conduct a thorough examination of the bodies. His scrutiny was professional; among all this remarkable man's accomplishments, he excelled in the field of surgery and medicine, for this had been his first training, his most intensive.

The examination completed, Doc entered the amusement park and went to the round building which housed the exhibition of prehistoric monsters. He did not go in boldly, but looked around and made sure none of the Tananese remained in the park. Those who had been disabled by the mercy bullets had been carried away by their fellows in their furtive exodus, for none of them were to be found.

Just inside the door of the circular structure, Doc plucked some of the artificial grasses, bundling the tips together tightly; then he scraped some dry, green cotton which had been glued to the boles of the great ferns to simulate moss, and shoved it into his improvised torch, after which he applied a match.

It was an unearthly scene which this torch lighted up, for in the fitful red flicker, the unearthly surroundings took on an unnatural reality, and the jumping luminance made the monsters seem alive, hideous. Their tooth-snaggled heads had the appearance of bobbing hungrily, jaws agape, as if in search of prey, while the green, unhealthy artificial jungle acquired an air of latent menace.

Smoke crawled upward from the firebrand, curling into eerie designs, twining and untwining, and the reeds popped and cackled as they were consumed. The moss fell away as it burned, making it necessary for Doc to turn back often and stamp out the red-hot threads, lest they fire the place.

Doc came suddenly upon two forms, enwrapped in canvas. They lay just inside the front door. One was large, bulky, as if it enclosed the frame of the apish chemist, Monk; and the other was thinner, a bit longer, as though Ham were inside.

Doc Savage looked at them for some moments, and there came into existence the small, fantastic trilling note which was the characteristic thing of the man of bronze in moments of stress or surprise.

The trilling note, tiny and unnatural, was oddly in keeping with his grotesque surroundings. And its undulating tune might have been the song of some prehistoric creature housed here in this fabulous spot. The trilling died finally, and Doc, stooping swiftly, stripped the canvas back from the objects they covered.

Inside were only two dummies, made up rather carefully of sticks and rolls of old sailcloth.

Chapter 11

HORROR IN GREEN

Police sirens were screaming on the hilltop above the amusement park, and Doc Savage left hastily, gliding down to the water and using his fabulous strength to launch the speedboat. He was so far out on the river before the first officer entered the park that the presence of the speedboat was not connected with the three dead men by the gate.

The Hudson was wide at that point, and Doc used binoculars, a pair of which were pocketed in the unusual speedboat to study the wharf before the Coastal Yacht Club. He saw standing upon the wharf the Khan Nadir Shar, tall and exotic in appearance, even from that distance; and behind the Khan, the sprawled forms that were the girl, Joan Lyndell, and bleached, brown Tananese. The latter were still unconscious from the effects of the chemical-salt shrapnel, but the Khan must have escaped the stuff.

Doc Savage did not send the speedboat across to the wharf, but only studied the scene through the binoculars long enough to become certain that no police had come upon the abandoned yacht club, a fact that was not remarkable considering that the club was on a section of the river front little frequented at this season of the year.

Doc went downstream, crossed to the Manhattan shore and tied up at the point at which he had left his car.

The mysterious thin man who had been rescued from the Tananese at the refinery was still in the car, unconscious from the drug which Doc had administered, his attitude surprisingly like that of a sleeping man, and Doc went over his clothing, something he had done before. He did it more thoroughly now.

The garments were costly, and had been fashioned by a tailor in Shanghai, China. There was nothing in the man's pockets, nor concealed in seams or lining of his clothing.

Doc got a case out of the car-door pocket, filled a hypo needle with a dark fluid and emptied it into the sleeping man's arm. The fellow then stirred and began to show life, sitting up finally. He did not speak for a long time; when he

76

did, his words were clear, his sentence structure coherent.

"What quaint methods you use," he said dryly.

"Want to talk?" Doc asked.

"Loquacity was always a failing of mine," the stranger smiled. "What shall we discuss? The weather? Rather chilly, what?"

Doc's weird flake-gold eyes rested unmoving upon the man's face, and the fellow, for the first time, showed a trace of uneasiness.

"I can administer drugs which will cause you to talk," Doc told him. "That may be necessary."

The man bowed slightly. "I believe I remarked that your methods are quaint."

"It is possible you are keeping quiet because you misunderstand the situation," Doc told him.

The stranger studied Doc's bleached features intently.

"You are aiding Joan Lyndell?" he asked. "Is that right?"

Doc watched the man's face. It was as devoid of expression as any he had ever seen, and Doc had made an intensive study of the tricks emotions play on faces.

"So far," Doc said, "I have only been endeavoring to aid my men. I was thrust into this. There has been no explanation of what it is all about."

"Are you going to help Joan Lyndell?" asked the man.

"I help only those who deserve it," Doc countered.

The man said jerkily, "Then you will not help her."

"Why not?"

"She is the Mystic Mullah," said the stranger bluntly.

Doc put questions, but the stranger closed up and fell back upon his facetious manner of answering questions. He remarked that the air was bracing; that he was hungry; that the river was beautiful with the morning sun upon it—and he would not commit himself beyond that.

He did not try to get out of the car as Doc drove north toward the abandoned yacht club. He refused twice to give his name. But that information was forthcoming when they reached the yacht club.

The Khan Nadir Shar came striding to meet Doc. The tattooed serpent design was brazen upon the Oriental potentate's forehead, and he looked very healthy, very powerful.

The Khan did not see the thin man in Doc's car until he was close. Sight of the fellow caused him to wrench up abruptly. His hand drifted to a pocket, flicked in, and came out with a gun which he must have taken from one of the unconscious Tananese.

"So you succeeded," he said distinctly, carefully.

"What do you mean?" Doc asked.

The Khan bobbed his hook-nosed head at the stranger.

"Oscar Gibson," he said.

"Is that his name?" Doc queried.

"It is," the Khan nodded.

"You know his business?" Doc demanded.

"Many men know that—to their sorrow," said the Khan. "This man is——"

"It's a damned lie!" Oscar Gibson rapped suddenly.

"This man is an agent of the Mystic Mullah!" continued the Khan.

"A lie!" exploded Gibson. "It cannot be proved!"

The Khan's forehead grew red and angry around the tattoo mark which marked him as the divinely ordained ruler of Tanan, a monarch who possessed absolute power over his subjects, as had his royal ancestors for many generations before him.

"This man knows who the Mystic Mullah is—if the creature is actually a living being, or perhaps I should say, living beast," the Khan said crisply. "It was in my capital city of Tanan that suspicion first shadowed his path, and my soldiers seized him. He told them he was an agent of the Mystic Mullah. Then he—escaped."

Oscar Gibson made a snarling sound. His hands whipped to his breast and tore at his shirt and undershirt. Opening them, his chest was revealed. His torso was hideous. Instead of skin, there was a nodular expanse of scar tissue.

"Coals from camp fires," gritted Gibson. "They dropped them on me, glowing red-hot, one at a time! I told them what they wanted to hear, not the truth."

"My chief, Mihafi, was in charge of the soldiers who seized you," the Khan told Gibson precisely. "Mihafi said there was no torture."

"A lie!" Gibson snapped. "Mihafi lied!"

Doc Savage looked at Gibson intently.

"A few minutes ago, you gave me the name of the person who is the Mystic Mullah," he said. "Have you any proof of that?"

"Only conviction," said Gibson; "nothing else."

The Khan's voice became suddenly shrill.

"Who did he name?" he demanded.

Doc Savage seemed not to hear, but walked toward the yacht club and around it until he saw the girl, Joan Lyndell.

They worked together, the three men, transferring Joan Lyndell and the Tananese into the yacht club, for it was possible that some curious person might sight the prone, motionless forms, if they were left outside, and call the police.

Doc Savage administered restoratives to the bleached, brown men in quick succession, first tying them securely, so that they could not move about. After all of the Tananese were conscious and fastened, Doc revived the girl.

There was something admirable in the way the young woman recovered from her period of senselessness, for she was not at all hysterical, and did not speak until she had full command of her faculties.

Oscar Gibson looked closely at Doc Savage, then away in such a manner that his glance conveyed meaning.

"A remarkable young woman," he said pointedly.

Doc Savage began speaking. His voice was quiet. He showed by no mannerism that he was perturbed, or that he was concerned over the fact that all five of his aides were in the hands of the Mystic Mullah's followers. He told of what had happened in the amusement park across the river.

"Now," he finished, "who is the Mystic Mullah?"

The Khan Nadir Shar bowed his head slightly. "A devil, a fiend such as your white man's hell, or the *mot ghalat* of my people, never produced! The Mystic Mullah is a menace to my subjects, to myself, to all of the world!"

"Be specific," Doc requested.

The girl took up the explanation.

"Years ago, my father went to Tanan," she said. "He was the first white man to come there, and the only white man ever permitted to live there. He was a trader, and he established a trading organization, building it until it spread over Tanan and the surrounding desert and mountains. Four years ago he died, and——"

"Made you probably the richest woman in the world," Oscar Gibson interjected bluntly. He wheeled upon Doc Savage. "She has more money than any two of your rich men put together. She may be the wealthiest person alive."

Joan Lyndell eyed the young man coldly.

"You have insufferable manners," she told him. "I wish I knew who you are."

"He is an agent of the Mystic Mullah," snapped the Khan.

"A lie!" yelled Gibson.

"We were talking about the Mystic Mullah," Doc suggested.

Joan Lyndell turned her back on Gibson. There was a composure about her manner, an easy sureness.

"More than a year ago, we first heard of the Mystic Mullah," she said. "A man was found dead in the street, a wealthy man, one holding a high position in my trading company. Not until weeks later did we learn that this man had been driven distraught by the apparition of a hideous green face which would appear at night, demanding money of him and threatening death unless he complied.

"The sums demanded were tremendous! The man was a millionaire, compared with American money, but complying with the demands would have left him a pauper. Obviously, he was killed because he refused."

The Khan Nadir Shar said abruptly, in a voice in which emotion was thick: "We speak only of the rich. It is not for them I worry. Let us speak of the poor, my subjects who have died since that day, a year past, when the Mystic Mullah first struck."

Joan Lyndell nodded.

"We began to hear of the Mystic Mullah," she said. "The stories were horrible—of men who died with fantastic green serpents, the green soul slaves of the Mystic Mullah, crawling over them. And the souls of these men became slaves of the Mystic Mullah. We do not know how many have died. Perhaps a thousand; perhaps more. But there has been enough that all of Tanan is terrified, and none dare mention the Mystic Mullah in public."

"Aimless killing?" Doc asked.

Joan Lyndell shook her head. "On the contrary, it has a very definite purpose. Only those who do not believe the Mystic Mullah is a supernatural power, not human at all, are the victims. In other words, the Mystic Mullah is building himself up an invisible empire founded on terror.

"Countless thousands of Tananese do his slightest bidding, or the bidding of those who are his subjects, because they fear not to do so. There are deaths every day. Always, they are the same. They are stricken in the night, or the darkness. They are heard screaming. Sometimes those who rush to them see hideous green things about them, but these vanish, and the victims are left with broken necks, always."

The young woman was speaking slightly bookish English, an indication that she had conversed in a foreign language so much that she found her mother tongue a bit awkward.

"There is talk that I am to be overthrown," the Khan Nadir Shar put in grimly. "There is to come a day when the Mystic Mullah will take my life with these things he calls his green soul slaves. And, later, he will spread his domain over all of Asia, and perhaps beyond."

Oscar Gibson, looking steadily at Doc Savage, asked, "How much of it do you believe?"

John Lyndell glared at him. "You are calling me a liar!"

Gibson scowled at her.

"I'll call you anything I please, my dear young lady," he advised. "The billion or so dollars that you are worth does not overawe me."

"You will keep quiet until you are called on," Doc told him.

Gibson smiled thinly, fiercely. "Do not let yourself be taken in," he said.

The Khan, as if to end the bickering, resumed: "Terror has seized all of Tanan. You cannot realize what horror has come over my people. They are distraught. This monster, this Mystic Mullah, is like an invisible demon, striking down all who oppose him, demanding gifts of money, of arms, and slaying through the medium of his green soul slaves those who refuse."

"Unless you know the Orient, it is difficult to understand how such a thing could happen," said Joan Lyndell. "In Tannan, the people are superstitious. For centuries, they have kept white men out, which was all the more difficult because Tanan is one of the richest countries in the world. It is a strange land, where firearms are still almost unknown, and where the sword and the lance are the standard fighting weapon."

She paused and studied Doc Savage, as if wondering how much belief he attached to the somewhat fantastic story she was telling.

"My own holdings in Tanan are endangered by the Mystic Mullah," she said. "Many of my most faithful men have perished. I know, to an absolute certainty, that I myself shall die unless the monster is stopped."

She began speaking more rapidly.

"We discussed many methods of fighting the Mystic Mullah," she said. "I am wealthy. The Khan is rich—according to American standards. We could have imported an army, but we were afraid it would not work. The Mystic Mullah can amass thousands of men, and the mountain passes into Tanan would withstand the most modern army. We could have used airplanes, except that there are few suitable fields.

"But, too"—she spread her hands—"the Mystic Mullah is only a name, a hideous green face in the night, a face no one has been able to touch, nor to harm, although I personally have emptied a revolver into it. How could an army fight something like that? So we came for you."

"I had heard of you," said the Khan. "Your fame is such, Doc Savage, that it has reached even remote Tanan."

He said this bombastically, in a manner that under circumstances less grim would have been faintly reminiscent of a politician passing out flattery.

"We took every precaution to keep our destination a secret," added the girl. "But it doesn't seem to have done any good."

Oscar Gibson squinted at her. His expression was skeptical; his whole manner one of disbelief, not of the story being told, but of the sincerity of the young woman herself.

"You are very concerned over the fate of your wealth," he said dryly.

The girl eyed him with utter coldness. "I am interested in the capture of the Mystic Mullah for another reason," she said.

Gibson lifted his brows. "Yes?"

"Yes," Joan Lyndell said steadily. "When my father died, his neck was found broken; and there was no mark upon his body, nor was there any conceivable explanation of how his neck had snapped."

Oscar Gibson started slightly, opened his mouth, shut it, then slowly moistened his lips. He began looking intently at the floor.

Doc Savage glanced at Gibson, as if on the point of questioning him; but something about the man's expression caused the bronze man to turn away and bend above one of the bound Tananese.

It was gloomy in the room, due partially to the boarded windows, but due also to the fact that the morning, which had started out so clear and cool, was changing, after the manner of New York weather, clouds springing up magically out of nowhere and settling over the bright sun and sinking like a fog into the deep cut through which the Hudson ran.

The Tananese only glared at the bronze man. Doc addressed him in the dialect of Tanan, speaking it so perfectly that the Khan showed surprise and the young woman gave him a sharp glance.

"Who is the one who calls himself the Mystic Mullah?" Doc asked.

The Tananese answered promptly, insultingly.

"A faithful dog knows his master," he said.

"And it is a wise dog which finds a new master when the old one can no longer care for him," Doc replied.

The Tananese shrugged, clipped his lips together and shut his eyes. He lay perfectly still, his whole attitude that of one absolutely determined not to speak and resigned to whatever fate befell him as a consequence.

Doc turned to another prisoner, but did not address him immediately. Instead, he sank beside the man and remained there, motionless. After a bit, he drew from a pocket a small flat case and held it where the Tananese could see it.

The case held only a lock-picking device and other small implements, none of them dangerous, but the prisoner did not know that and, judging from his expression, used his imagination to picture some lethal horror inside the case.

The Khan Nadir Shar came over and said solemnly, "You cannot persuade these men to talk. They are from a mountain tribe of Tanan, a fierce, utterly cruel clan which has been a source of terror for centuries."

"Human nature is very much the same the world over," Doc told the Khan. "Watch him break down."

The bronze man held the shiny case closer to the eyes of the Tananese captive, forcing the man to look at it with an unwinking intentness. So softly that its presence was at first scarcely noticeable, the bronze man's fantastic trilling note eased out of nothingness and began to trace its exotic notes. It was a pæan of utter unreality, and it had a marked effect upon the Tananese. The fellow stared. He breathed loudly.

What Doc Savage was doing smacked of black magic, but the explanation was simple; he was slowly building up a hypnotic spell. Once hypnotized, the Tananese might be induced to talk.

But his plan was never completed.

Oscar Gibson shrilled suddenly, "Watch out! Across the room!"

Doc Savage looked up. Hideous green things were coming toward him. They were almost transparent; he could see completely through some of the thinner ones. They averaged as long as his arm, but some were thin as ropes, others almost as thick as Doc's vast chest.

"The green souls!" gasped the girl, Joan Lyndell.

Springing to the side and backward, the young woman swooped and picked up an automatic from the pile of weapons which had been taken from the captured Tananese. Oscar Gibson saw her move, lunged as if to seize her. The young woman began shooting at the green horrors. Gibson veered away from her, got one of the guns and himself began firing. The smashing of the guns was ear-splitting.

The emerald things were not visibly affected by the bullets. They came along the floor, some seeming to crawl on the dusty planks, others a few inches in the air. Their color blended surprisingly with the darkness; at times they were almost invisible.

They reached the first bound captive and he emitted an awful shriek and threshed about. The olivaceous, serpentine bodies squirmed on. They did not travel smoothly. At times they jerked about. Again, they almost stopped. They piled together and seemed to merge into larger corporeities.

There were more of them now. Hundreds! They danced across the floor like fantastic dervishes, like evil harpies creeping out of some cavernous lair on the other side of the vast room, where it was too dark to distinguish details.

Joan Lyndell and Oscar Gibson had emptied their guns by now. And they had done no good.

"Get out of here!" the girl cried loudly. "They cannot be harmed!"

She began to retreat. The Khan followed her, hands out before him as if to ward off the incredible green bodies.

Doc Savage, instead of going back toward the door and the outside, advanced. He bent forward a little. His flake-gold eyes strained to view the green things more closely.

Oscar Gibson yelled, "Careful! If you touch them, they'll kill you!"

Doc Savage did not answer. He picked up a fragment of trash from the floor, threw it. The missile went entirely through the largest of the absinthe-tinted things, causing a minor disturbance in its body.

Doc got a second piece of trash, a lump of plaster. He stepped close, threw again. He was trying to fathom the mystery of the things. But the light was insufficient. He raced fingers through his pockets, searching for matches.

So intent was Doc Savage upon the green horror he was investigating that he did not note that other olive-hued things were banking close on either side, threatening to cut off his retreat to the door.

The prisoners were screaming now, shrieking as if their very souls were coming out. And as they were touched by the serpentine marauders, they began to writhe about in the throes of death agony. The necks of the first to be affected were already beginning to jerk, to snap about as if in the grip of invisible giants.

Doc Savage abandoned his investigation of the fat green

body and swung to the nearest prisoner. He scooped the fellow up, got him across a shoulder; then got two more of the captives, one under either arm.

He took two paces toward the door—stopped. The green things had moved to the wall, shutting off retreat. He was trapped.

The horrors were closing in. There were more hundreds of them. The whole room seemed to have turned green.

One drifted toward Doc Savage. He whipped down, to the side. One of the Tananese he was carrying contorted and managed to get his bound legs underfoot. Tripped, Doc sank to a knee. The other two Tananese began to kick and flail about. It was obvious that they did not want to be rescued.

Doc dropped them. There was nothing else to do. He needed all his agility to escape the green things. He worked backward. One of the serpentine objects came close; Doc ducked, and it all but touched him. Sliding backward, he was almost against another. They were on all sides.

One of the Tananese was yelling, "Watch the green soul slaves of our master overcome this white devil ghost!"

Again and again, Doc tried to reach the door. Each time, he was cut off. He sprang high into the air. He got down and crawled. He tried battering holes in the plaster with his fists, hoping to break through the wall. But he encountered a wall of thick planks. Evidently the yacht club building had been enlarged long ago.

The bronze man was breathing noisily now. It was one of the few times in his life that he had been trapped with no avenue of escape at hand. His present position seemed hopeless. He began to wrench off his coat, to rip off the sleeves, to cover his hands, his face.

Then there was a shout from the door. Oscar Gibson came leaping inside. He carried an old sail, a fragment of twelve-ounce duck fully a dozen feet square.

"Watch it!" he shouted, and flung the sail out before him.

The effect was surprising. The green things were caught by the sail, borne down, whipped aside. Gibson skidded the sail forward, whipped it up again and literally fanned the green things aside.

"Now!" he barked.

There was no need for the suggestion. Doc Savage was leaping through the space the fanning sail had cleared. Together, he and Gibson reached the door and gained the outside.

"Thanks," Doc Savage said quietly.

Gibson grinned, said nothing.

"Let's try the other side of the club," Doc rapped. "Those things came from somewhere!"

They ran through the soft mud, splashing and slipping, reached the end of the old yacht club and sloped around. They skidded to a stop and stared.

A giant of a man stood before them, a fellow with a vast frame and tremendous bones and little flesh to spare, a man who had a pair of fists so huge that they seemed out of proportion, even when compared to his huge form. He was busy tearing a gag out of his mouth with hands that bore ugly red welts, as if they had been seared with hot irons. There were more of the welts across his face.

"Holy cow!" he boomed when he had the gag out.

It was Renny, Doc's big-fisted engineer aide.

Chapter 12

ASIATIC EXODUS

Doc Savage ran on past Renny without speaking, rounded another corner and studied the rear of the yacht club. The ground seemed, if anything, more muddy than it had before. The soft muck bore tracks—some made earlier in the morning, but some also that had undoubtedly been imprinted within the last few moments. These led to a side door; the same tracks led away.

Doc whirled. His eyes ranged the terrain surrounding the yacht club. There was bare ground—not mud—for some distance, but beyond that there was grass, then foliage of the park which flanked the Hudson at this point. Most of the landscaped vegetation was bare of leafage; but here and there stood an evergreen, and these were profuse enough to furnish cover.

Inside the yacht club, the shrieks were dying away in frightful fashion.

Doc ran back to where Renny stood.

"How many brought you here from the amusement park?" he demanded.

"Three or four," Renny boomed.

"The Mystic Mullah with them?"

"Darned if I know," said Renny. "They got into the yacht club through a back door. Then they came out, ran off and left me. I was tied up and it took me a little time to get loose."

He indicated a spot in the mud where lay lengths of ordinary cotton clothes line, and added, "I was tied with that stuff."

Doc Savage whipped away, found the trail made by the departing party which had brought Renny, and followed it. The tracks were distinct through the mud, even more distinct beyond, for mud had scraped off shoes onto grass.

The prints processioned up a hill, took shelter behind evergreens, went on, and eventually reached a path. There they were lost to anything but an extraordinary eye. Doc Savage managed to follow them up to the wall that topped the cliff, edging Riverside Drive.

Cars whizzed steadily on the drive. Taxicabs cruised. There was no hope of trailing the Tananese further. They could have taken a cab; they might have had their own car waiting. Doc went back and joined Renny. He found the big-fisted engineer and Oscar Gibson glaring at each other.

"One more squawk out of you and I'll pound you down into the ground to your hips!" Renny was telling Gibson fiercely.

Gibson sneered. "I still say it is suspicious."

Doc asked, "What is wrong now?"

"This snipe," Renny jabbed a fist at Gibson. "This snipe thinks it was funny because them brown geezers turned me loose. He up and said so."

"The Mystic Mullah's assistants are not in the habit of freeing their prisoners," Gibson said nastily.

Renny boomed, "They turned me loose for a danged good reason."

"What was it?" Doc asked.

"They've got Long Tom and Johnny," Renny said grimly. "They're taking both of them to Tanan. They've already chartered planes, and they're going to take off immediately, carrying Long Tom and Johnny along."

"How do you know this?" Gibson interjected.

"They told me," Renny rumbled. "They also told me to tell Doc."

Gibson snapped, "I do not understand why they should do that."

"They were bald-faced enough about it," Renny told him. "The Mystic Mullah has got enough of Doc. He don't care about fighting him any more here in New York. He's simply grabbed two of Doc's men and carried them off to decoy Doc into Tanan, where the Mullah can fight on his own ground. It's not a new gag."

Joan Lyndell and the Khan Nadir Shar came around the yacht club, and their faces were horrified and they walked as if in trances.

"The prisoners in the club," the girl said hoarsely, "are all dead!"

Doc Savage said nothing; he might have been expecting the news. Nor did Oscar Gibson show that it was other than he expected.

Doc asked Renny, "How did they get you in that amusement park?"

"We barged into that prehistoric world exhibit, thinking we were going to rescue Monk and Ham," the engineer rumbled, and swung his big fists angrily. "The green snakes got us."

He pointed at the ugly red welts across his hands and face.

"Whenever the things touched us, it was as if they were red-hot irons," he continued. "They burned like fire. We couldn't fight them off. And after while, we all passed out."

Oscar Gibson said incredulously, "But the green soul slaves usually kill their victims."

"They didn't kill us," Renny pointed out. "They just burned us, and we passed out. Then we woke up with headaches and feeling kinda weak. We were bound and gagged. The guys who held us told me what to tell Doc, then brought me here. That's all I know."

"Any sign of Monk and Ham?" Doc asked.

"No," Renny said slowly. "And that was bad. Those fellows did not say a word about them. They talked like they were going to take only Johnny and Long Tom with them."

"You asked them about Monk and Ham?" Doc queried.

Renny nodded. "And they just gave me the ugly eye."

After that, silence fell, for Doc Savage seemed to have nothing more to say, and Renny did not speak further. Side by side, they swung slowly toward the door of the yacht club. Their steps were slow, and one knowing them would have realized that they were enwrapped in a shroud of gloom, of grief, believing as they did that the actions of the brown men of Tanan had indicated that both Monk and Ham were dead.

It was hideous news, and the consideration of it steeped them in sorrow. Monk and Ham had been associated with them for years. They had gone through incredible perils together, had saved each other's lives on occasion, and had been amused always by the friendly bickering between Monk and Ham, the quarrel that never died.

Doc reached the door. Inside, bodies sprawled in the gloom. They were contorted in grisly fashion, and their heads hung as if their necks had been emptied of bones.

"Necks broken," Renny said thickly. "It's incredible! What infernal thing does it, Doc?"

The bronze man did not reply. He entered the room, stepping cautiously, eyes alert for some sign of the green horrors that were like ghostly snakes. But none of the things were to be seen. They had vanished as inexplicably as they had come.

Renny spoke again, hoarsely: "There's no need of hanging around here, Doc. Let's get on the trail of Johnny and Long Tom. Those fellows may have taken off in their planes by now."

Doc nodded. "We will follow them. That is what they wanted; but it is the only thing we can do."

The bronze man moved toward one of the doors that led deeper into the old yacht club structure.

"What are you going to do?" Renny demanded.

"Search the place," Doc said. "We have had no time to do that. We might find something."

Renny started to object, then silenced himself, realizing what Doc meant by "something"—the bodies of Monk and Ham, perhaps. They began to go through rooms that were littered with rubble, to pry into closets which held old yachting caps, discarded white ducks, broken oars, old sails and even a rusted, worthless outboard motor.

They came to a closet which was very dark, and Doc stepped inside, scraping a match alight. Renny waited outside. Suddenly, he stiffened.

Doc's trilling had piped out, short, surprised, more violent than was its usual note. It lasted only a brief moment. Renny lunged forward.

Two forms were sprawled in the closet. Doc was untying them, and they were kicking about, very much alive.

"Monk!" Renny exploded. "Ham!"

The homely Monk, his mouth ridded of the gag, grinned, "Them brown guys were chased off before they had time to move us. Boy, I began to think you'd never find us!"

His hands and face were covered with the same type of red welts which decorated Renny's fists and features. Ham bore the same markings.

Ham, with the gag out of his mouth, spat violently and demanded, "Where's my sword cane?"

Chapter 13

THE SECRET SERVICE MAN

The time was two days later.

The plane had three motors, each of them supercharged with nearly a thousand horse power and all labored in unison, hurling the big ship ahead at a speed which very seldom fell below two hundred miles an hour. A time or two, when the ship was very high, seeking out stratospheric air currents that were favorable, the speed had been far above three hundred an hour.

The wings of the ship were streamlined into the fuselage; the landing wheels drew up in the hull, also shaped so as to serve as a big pontoon for landing on water; and nowhere did a strut or a brace wire show outside the streamlining.

It was quiet in the cabin, almost unnaturally so. The brawl of the big engines was but a peaceful murmur. The silencing job on that cabin was remarkable. Aëronautical engineers had come from some of the world's most advanced plants to inspect it.

It was warm in the cabin, too; warm, although there was snow below, vast whitenesses of it. It seemed as if the plane had shifted to another world, for there were no rivers visible on this terrain below, no mountains. There was only smooth whiteness.

Had the ship dropped to a lower altitude, however, the ground would have taken on some resemblance to an earthly domain, for this was tundra below, the amazing expanse of near-swamp which covers parts of Siberia.

Renny was at the plane controls, nursing the air-speed meter, endeavoring to get it up a bit higher without racing the motors unnecessarily.

Monk and Ham, as usual, were quarreling.

"You missing link!" Ham snarled. "I'll cut you open and see if you look any more like a human inside than you do on the outside!"

The slender, waspish lawyer carried a sword cane, not the one with which he had started out to investigate the tug *Whale of Gotham* in New York, for that one had been lost.

This weapon was one from a stock of spares which Ham kept in his club apartment.

Monk, the homely chemist, scowled fiercely at Ham.

"Just a big mouth and a lot of noise," he sneered. "You keep your hands off that hog, or I'll give you a good wringing and hang you up to dry."

Between the two belligerents, an interested observer to the argument, was Monk's pet pig, Habeas Corpus. Habeas had been named in a manner calculated to aggravate Ham. He was a remarkable specimen of the porker race, this Habeas Corpus. He was predominately ears, with a generous proportioning of snout and legs, the rest of him being thin and scrawny.

Habeas Corpus and Monk had joined company in Arabia so many months ago that it was by now evident that the shote would never grow much larger. He ate prodigiously without gaining an ounce. But Habeas had also demonstrated that, as a mental specimen, he was no ordinary porker. He learned tricks with the ease of a show dog, and Monk spent most of his spare time training the shote.

The immediate cause of Monk and Ham's quarrel was certain damage Habeas Corpus had done to Ham's immaculate traveling bag. Habeas had gnawed practically the entire end out of the cowskin bag.

"Habeas don't like cows," Monk explained. "When you pick your next bag, don't have it made of cowskin."

"It'll probably be pigskin," Ham gritted, and eyed Habeas meaningly.

The plane hit a down current and pitched sickeningly, so that they all were forced to grasp the arm rests of the seats to retain their positions.

"Such flying," Ham said.

Renny called, "You start razzing me and I'll pick your arms and legs off."

The Khan Nadir Shar looked on with drowsy interest. He had been a long time without sleep and he seemed on the point of dropping off.

Joan Lyndell sat across from Oscar Gibson, and they both looked straight ahead, neither giving attention to the other or even acting as if the other existed.

Renny made some calculations, put figures and words on a paper and passed it back.

"There's our position," he advised. "We'll have to land in Novo Sibirsk for refueling."

Doc Savage, secluded in the rear of the plane, received the

message without comment, read it, then advised, "Better radio ahead so that gasoline will be ready."

"You think the Mystic Mullah's men are still ahead of us?" Renny called.

"That is difficult to say," Doc replied. "They had fast planes."

Doc and his men had made inquiries before taking off from New York and had learned that two planes laden with the brown men of Tanan had actually taken off from a Gotham airport. The ships had been heard from in Nova Scotia; they had landed in Iceland, and had refueled at the point of guns. Next word of them had come from Finland, where they had again refueled by force. It was that phantom trail which Doc Savage was following.

That the Tananese were still ahead, Doc had reason to believe, for his own ship, delayed in starting some hours, had hit bad weather which the other craft must have missed. The North Atlantic had been disturbed, and there had been head winds, even up into the lower stratosphere as far as the big speed plane could penetrate.

The bronze man closed the door of the compartment in the rear of the plane and continued what he had been doing —taking his exercises. These exercises, over a period of years, were entirely responsible for his amazing physical development. He had been taking them now for almost two hours, and not yet was he done. He had gone through the same intensive routine each day since childhood. Not only did Doc develop his muscles, but his five senses as well, using complicated apparatus for that purpose.

The aluminum hue lent by the chemical bleaching agent had faded, allowing Doc's bronze color to return.

Doc was completing his exercises when the plane tilted sharply and the changed note of the motors indicated a descent. He left the compartment and went forward.

"Novo Sibirsk," Renny said.

Novo Sibirsk, situated on the navigable Ob River, was a typical metropolis of southern Siberia. The river was off to the left now, with its nine spans plainly distinguishable, and the thin thread of the trans-Siberian railway stretching away into the infinite distance. There were large buildings below, grain elevators and flour mills, probably, and everywhere was a bright newness. Columns of smoke curled up from the iron smelting plants.

Renny cut the motors and opened the cabin windows in order to see better. At a very low altitude, they scudded over the fringe of the town. They were so low that the odor of a tannery was plainly distinguishable as they glided above it.

The airport appeared, its modernity a mark of the industrial efforts of the Soviets. The hangars were substantial, and snowplows had boosted the field clear of deeper drifts. The air lashing in through the plane windows was bitterly cold.

Renny cranked the landing wheels out of their streamlined recesses and planted the ship with a skilled ease on the field. Whooping gusts from the propellers pulled the plane toward the hangars and the little flags on flexible staffs which marked the location of the gas tanks.

Renny cut the motors when close to the hangars. In the silence, the snow squealed under the wheels; it wailed louder when he applied the brakes, and the craft came to a stop.

Monk arose, stretched his furry arms and announced, "I'm gonna stoke the human machine with some food."

He opened the cabin door.

Out of the near-by hangar popped a squad of men. They held rifles. Obviously they had been concealed, awaiting the moment the plane would stop.

"Something wrong!" Renny rapped.

He snapped on the ignition switches, made passes at the starter buttons. The hot motors crashed into life. The plane veered around, began moving.

To the right, the left, on the front and rear, men sprang out of the huge piles of snow which tractors had pushed aside from the airport runways. They gripped the ends of thin wire cables. They yanked these, disclosing the fact the cables were buried in the snow. The men, tugging on them, got them waist-high and in the plane's path.

One cable snagged across the landing wheels, high enough that it was above the streamlined pants, where it would not slip off.

"They can't hold us!" Renny boomed.

He was wrong. The men did not depend on physical strength alone to hold the plane; for they tied the ends of the wire cables around steel rods which had been previously driven into the frozen earth.

There was a jar as the plane snubbed against the lines. The cable gave a little, the spring effect cushioning the shock of the stoppage. Then the big ship lay helpless.

The uniformed men dashed forward, rifles slanted across their chests. There was military precision in their movements.

They wore the metal helmets of the Soviet military, with knitted winter covers over the helmets and protecting their ears from the bitter cold. Their overcoats were very long, their boots huge. There was not an unshaven face among them.

The leader trotted up alongside the plane door and lifted his voice.

"You will come out," he said in excellent English. "You are under arrest!"

Monk angrily hauled down a window and demanded, "Just what the hades is the meaning of this?"

"We have orders to search your plane," imparted the Soviet officer. "It has been reported that you have been taking pictures of Soviet fortified areas."

"Is that all you intend to do—search the plane?" Doc Savage put in.

"Yes," said the officer.

"Go ahead," Doc told him. "But what I should like to know is what instigated this. Who reported we had been taking pictures?"

"A cablegram came from Omsk," advised the Soviet commandant. "It was signed merely by one who called himself a 'Friend of the Soviet'."

Monk breathed, so only Doc could hear the words, "The Mystic Mullah!"

The Soviet soldiers entered the plane and directed all of the occupants outside. Their manner was firm without being roughshod; they kept their rifles ready, but did not aim them.

The commanding officer and two assistants did the searching. They went through each item of baggage, not scattering the contents, but carefully repacking after examination. They came to the last of the items of baggage without finding anything. After that, they began going over the plane itself, carefully prying at wall paneling to see if it had been loosened recently. They found nothing.

Two men clambered out on the wings and opened the large caps of the gas tanks. Flashlights were brought and thrust down into the apertures.

"*Shto'!*" exploded one in his native tongue. "*E'ta tako'ye?* What is that?"

They tried to fish in the tank, but the opening was too small. Finally, they summoned a small boy, and the urchin, peeling his sheepskin *koortka*, inserted a thin arm into the tank and brought it out dripping gasoline and triumphantly clutching a long glass bottle in which was a curl of photographic prints.

The officer examined these.

"Bes samneneeye!" he said grimly. "Without a doubt! These are photographic prints of some of our fortified area."

Monk yelled, "Say guy, there's something screwy———"

"You will have a chance to tell it at the trial," the Soviet officer said grimly.

The jail was very modern, except for the heating arrangement. It was bitterly cold in the large, white cell. The naked walls echoed back the steady tramping of a sentry somewhere down the corridor.

Monk, a gloomy expression on his homely features, sat on a low bench and scratched the ears of Habeas Corpus, his pet pig.

"There ain't no doubt of it," he said, disgust in his small voice. "Back there at one of them places we got gasoline, somebody put that glass jar of pictures into the gas tank. Some airport attendant was bribed to do the job. If this ain't a swell note!"

Ham requested unkindly, "Will you shut up! We can all guess what happened. But the important thing is—what to do about it?"

Monk went on as if he had not heard. "That picture business is the fine hand of this Mystic Mullah. There ain't no doubt about that, either. Say, what do these Soviets do with spies? Do they shoot 'em?"

"Shooting is employed only in time of war," Doc told him dryly. "They usually send them to Siberian prison camps for thirty or forty years."

"Pleasant thought," Monk muttered.

Oscar Gibson stood to one side, against the barred door of the cell, and watched the pacing sentry. Gibson had said little. As a matter of fact, he had spoken only when necessary since they had left New York. Not that he had been left alone, for Monk, Ham and Renny, as well as Doc Savage, had had tries at questioning him. But Oscar Gibson, where information about himself was concerned, had the characteristics of a clam.

Just who Oscar Gibson was, what connection he had with the affair of the Mystic Mullah, was a complete mystery.

Monk lifted the pig, Habeas Corpus, by both ears and swung him back and forth, a procedure that Habeas seemed to enjoy immensely.

"What do you say, Doc—shall we try a break?" he demanded.

Doc Savage shook his head slowly. He was watching

Oscar Gibson, who still leaned against the barred door. The pacing sentry had stopped outside. He leaned close to the bars. Oscar Gibson said something. His voice was so low that it did not reach Doc Savage.

Then Gibson reached into his mouth and withdrew a bridge of false teeth, the first indication any of them had that some of his molars were artificial. He held the bridgework so that only the guard could see it.

The guard's start was plainly distinguishable. Gibson said something further, and they could tell only that he was speaking Russian fluently.

The guard whipped out a key and unlocked the barred door.

Monk came to life suddenly, dropped Habeas and lunged headlong for the door, hoping to bowl Gibson against the guard and thus open the way for an escape. But Gibson was too fast for him. He got through the door, slammed it, and the automatic lock clicked securely.

Monk took the force of his charge with a shoulder, bounced back, and glared at Gibson. "What's the idea, guy?" he growled.

"I believe the proper Yankee terminology is 'Nuts to you'," Gibson said airily.

Gibson marched away in company with the guard, and Monk stood for some moments by the door, grumbling to himself.

"Danged if I can make that guy Gibson out," Monk finally announced, disgustedly.

"He is a mysterious person," Joan Lyndell agreed.

"He is one of the Mystic Mullah's agents, I am convinced," rumbled the Khan Nadir Shar, and the tattooed serpent coiled around the jewel on his forehead, glowed redly with anger.

Doc Savage seemed to be listening.

"The guard went outside with Gibson!" he rapped. "Now is our chance!"

The bronze man flung to the window. This was a tunnellike opening through which very little light came, for the wall was fully five feet thick. The glass panes closing the window were at the outer extremity, so that prisoners could not reach them and use the glass for stabbing purposes.

The inner bars were almost an inch thick and bedded deeply in stone. Removing them was beyond the ability of naked hands, as Doc found out when he grasped them and wrenched; they barely groaned in their sockets.

The prisoners had been searched most thoroughly, the men being forced to remove their clothing in the process. But they had been given back their own garments.

Doc still wore his necktie. It was loose about his neck. He stripped it off, inserted a thumb in the large end and ripped it open. The lining was a yellowish, stiff cloth which looked like the usual lining put in neckties. Doc pulled the lining out.

He picked several buttons off his coat, including the ornamental ones on the sleeves. These crushed with surprising ease, became a brownish powder as he ground them between his corded fingers. He placed the powder along the necktie lining, as if he were making a cigarette of strange nature, then rolled the lining, inclosing the powder.

His movements became swifter. He tore the long cylinder he had made into four pieces. He bound these around the lower and upper ends of two bars.

"What on earth are you doing?" Joan Lyndell breathed wonderingly.

Monk grinned and cackled, "I get it! I get it!" He ran forward, fishing in a pocket.

"They left me one match," he chuckled. "That'll speed it up."

"It will," Doc agreed.

The bronze man struck Monk's match carefully, applied it to the yellow rolls of necktie lining, and the results were surprising. Came a loud hiss. The cell became blindingly white from the light of the burning substance. They all felt the tremendous heat.

Doc backed away and waited. The substance he had secured to the bars continued to hiss. It was burning with a violence that rivaled the heat of an electric torch. There was the same flickering. The light became too brilliant for their eyes and they squinted, covered their faces.

"What is it?" Joan Lyndell gasped.

"Ever hear of thermit?" Monk asked her.

"No."

"A mixture of aluminum powder and iron oxide," Monk told her. "It is used in welding, principally. That necktie lining was impregnated with the aluminum powder, and the buttons were the oxide. There were some other chemicals mixed in with it to make it more efficient than ordinary thermit. It generates a terrific heat when it burns."

Doc Savage was balling his coat about his hands, forming a pad. Using this as a protection, he lunged at the bars.

These were white hot at the ends, red in the middle, and were bending slightly of their own weight.

His impact against the first bar caused it to break. He knocked the second one out. Using the coat, he brushed the thermit and molten steel away, as much of it as he could. Then he threw the coat over the glowing bar ends, and before it burned through or burst into flame, scrambled over and got into the tunnellike aperture of the window.

He knocked the glass from the outer end. There was snow heaped on the sill. He scooped that up in his hands and used it to cool the bar ends so that the others could clamber up.

The prison, although its interior was modern, had been built centuries ago, possibly having once served as a fortress, for there was a moat surrounding the wall. This was now banked full of snow, and Doc Savage, dropping down, sank considerably over his head. Lying in the pit he had made, he looked upward and made sure there were no guards on the high walls.

The others followed him down. There was harder snow under the fluffy upper layer, and they managed to work across the moat and scramble out on the other side. They ran across a stretch of park where naked trees reared up around them, their hurried feet kicking up clouds of snow.

Some one yelled in Russian: *"Stoi! Stoi!"*

"This way!" Doc rapped. "They're yelling for us to halt."

The fugitives dived into a small creek which wound through the park and descended a hill toward the river Ob. This sheltered them. A few bullets searched them out with vicious squeals.

The Soviet prison guards yelled a few more *"Sois!"* and then began ringing a bell. The bell must have been tremendous. Its reverberations shuddered out and undoubtedly carried for miles.

The creek was frozen over, packed with snow; but here and there ice was uncovered. Monk, hitting one of these slick stretches with too much speed, slipped and fell, much to the discomfort of Habeas Corpus, whom he had thrust inside his coat for easier carrying. The pig began squealing.

"Knock him in the head," Ham suggested.

Monk only snorted.

They passed under a bridge, and the driver of a *kareta* crossing over the stone structure saw them, reined up and began to yell at the top of his voice. This frightened his wild Siberian ponies, and they promptly ran off, so that the driver's yells, if they were heard, would probably be construed as directed at his steeds.

"That was a lucky break!" Renny boomed.

They reached another bridge, climbed up beside it, and trotted down a road. A few moments later they saw the airport ahead, the hangars looking larger than they were because of the expanse of snow.

"Lookit!" Monk exploded. "I'll say we're getting the breaks. There's our plane, with the motors turning over!"

The big plane stood on the field, slightly away from the nearest hangar, in a position as convenient for their purpose as could have been wished for. The three propellers were spinning disks of alloy, and the exhaust stacks spilled occasional gusts of oil smoke.

"This can't be real!" Renny thumped.

They raced toward the plane. Eyes were alert. But no one appeared to head them off. No alarm was shouted.

Doc bounded into the plane, plunged forward to take the control bucket. The others piled into the cabin. Ham barked something unintelligible but glad when he discovered his sword cane reposing on the plane floor where he had left it. He pounced upon it. Monk clambered into the ship, carrying Habeas by one oversize ear, then banged the door.

Doc sawed the throttles open; the ship lifted its tail and nearly three thousand thundering horsepower sucked it across the field and up into the cold sunlight.

The windows were open, and Doc closed them. They were double-paneled, equipped to thwart frost formation and to keep out sound. The cabin became quiet as the interior of a hearse.

"Holy cow!" Renny rumbled gloomily. "We were nearly out of gas when we landed. What're we gonna do for fuel? We're still a good thousand miles from Tanan."

Doc said, "Have a look at this instrument panel, Renny."

The big-fisted engineer ambled forward, his long face wearing an expression slightly more sorrowful than usual—if that were possible—and eyed the board. At first, he caught nothing of significance. And then he saw.

"Fuel gauge!" he barked. "Our tanks are full!"

Joan Lyndell came up behind him and said, "That is strange! And isn't it unusual that we should find the plane at the airport with the engines running. It was as if it had been made ready for us."

"It was," said a new voice.

They whirled. The tone was distinct in the soundproofed cabin. They all recognized it.

Oscar Gibson, thin-waisted and narrow-lipped, stood in the rear of the cabin. His lips had a faint upward warp at the corners, and there was a small sparkle to his eyes. He had been stowed away in the rear compartment.

"I must say that I barely reached the airport in time to have them prepare the plane for you," he said dryly. "I felt sure, once word spread that you had escaped, that you would head for the airport. But how did you get out of that prison cell? It is supposed to be one of the strongest in Russia?"

Nobody answered him.

"*You* had this plane arranged for us?" Renny boomed unbelievingly.

Gibson bowed slightly. "I would have arranged your release, as well, if you had allowed me a little time."

"I don't believe you would've!" Monk snorted. "Just who are you, anyhow?"

Gibson inserted a little finger between his lips and worked out the bridge of false teeth. He turned this over, presenting the rather unusually wide gold bar for their inspection.

Engraved on the bar was a peculiar design. It incorporated the hammer and sickle of the Soviet. There were a few engraved words of Russian. Doc read them and studied the design.

"Secret Police," he said.

"Exactly," said Oscar Gibson. "I am a member. More correctly I am one of the four highest ranking officers."

"But you're English!" Monk exploded.

"I was born in Texas," Gibson said gravely. "Some day, when I get tired of adventuring, I shall go back there. In the meantime, I shall make every effort to stamp out one of the greatest curses ever afflicted upon the human race, the Mystic Mullah."

"You are working for the Soviet on this?" Doc asked.

Gibson nodded. "Secretly and without official public acknowledgment, of course. The Soviet wants peace in the Orient. This devil, the Mystic Mullah, is hungry for power. He is slowly taking over Tanan. He practically has it in the palm of his hand now. After Tanan will come Tibet, Afghanistan, Mongolia, China and, eventually, Russia."

"This thing must be big," Monk said slowly.

"It is," Gibson agreed. "Big—and horrible!"

Doc Savage turned back to the control wheel and the big plane pointed its baying snout at the sun and climbed toward the lower zone of stratosphere.

Chapter 14

THE HUMAN SPIDER

It is written that the Genghis Khan, mighty Mongol of the twelfth century, whose ferocious soldiers probably set the all-time record for slaughtering prisoners of war when they took a million and a half lives in a captured city, once pushed a campaign against Tanan, and failing to take it, beheaded those of his war chiefs who had been in charge of the campaign and had their graves marked with the legend:

These are fools, for they have butted a stone wall with their heads, yet they recognized the stone wall not until they had cast away a hundred thousand fighting men and more.

Had the violent Genghis returned from whatever after-life his deeds warranted him, and visited Tanan, he would probably have been more at home than any other spot on the globe, for Tanan was much as it had been in Genghis Khan's day. The soldiers still carried their short, fearful swords, wore quilted armor; and such guns as they had—and they had a few, for the Orient sired the invention of gunpowder—were unique relics, more cannon than rifle, requiring two men to carry them. They fired anything from a ball of copper pounded from the rich natural deposits in Tanan, to a fistful of pebbles, or, if a man were desperate, various oddly shaped Tananese coins.

Yet the arrival of Doc Savage's plane did not create the awe that might be expected, for it developed that Joan Lyndell kept two planes of her own, both speedy, marvelously appointed craft piloted by ex-army fliers from the Chinese Nationalist air force.

Doc Savage and his men were not in Tanan long before they began to realize that Joan Lyndell was a remarkable young woman indeed. In New York, and in the wild chase across the north Atlantic and over Russia, she had been but an extremely pretty bit of femininity who was rumored to have inherited a fortune from a wealthy trader father.

In Tanan, it developed, she was a power. Indeed, Doc Savage began to understand before long that she was actually more of an influence than the Khan Nadir Shar himself. Oscar Gibson, the remarkable young American who was a high Soviet secret service official, verified this.

"The girl dictates the Khan's policies of government," he advised. "The Khan is a nice enough old war horse, but he is no statesman. The girl could buy and sell him a dozen times. Her private force of company guards, organized to protect the caravans which she sends into the wild mountain regions to trade with the savage tribesmen, is a larger force than the Khan's own army, and better equipped."

"Yet you said she was the Mystic Mullah," Doc reminded him. "What made you say that?"

"I might have been mistaken. I will know when I find out if her father really died of a broken neck, like the Mystic Mullah's victims." After that, Gibson clipped his lips together tightly.

A band of Joan Lyndell's company guards met them at the young woman's private flying field. There were nearly four hundred of them, and they marched with a precision that aroused the appreciation of Renny, who had an eye for military things.

Joan Lyndell herself retired to the compartment at the rear of the plane, and when she reappeared, she wore the garb of a Tananese woman of royal descent. The attire was exotic, consisting of an embroidered satin jacket embellished with silver and gold, and a rather voluminous skirt, with a sash of incredibly brilliant green. There was a headdress equally as elaborate, a resplendent affair with jewels and entwining gold wire. And she had affixed rather enormous earrings to her ear lobes.

"You are a knockout!" Monk told her.

"When in Tanan, it is better to dress as the Tananese do," she said. "You would be well to take that advice yourselves."

Two hours later, Monk was holding his sides, laughing. His mirth was hysterical, and finally he sat down weakly.

"What the well-dressed lawyer will wear!" he choked. "What a picture you are!"

Ham scowled blackly. He had just donned the clothing of a Tananese gentleman, which consisted principally of more than a dozen square yards of coarse cloth draped about his person in folds. He had tried various methods of folding. Now he glared at Monk and demanded, "How do they keep these things on?"

"Darned if I know," Monk told him. "I used safety pins."

A part of their equipment, they discovered, was a short sword, and they had noted that the Tananese wore these, not in the conventional fashion dangling at the side, but strapped directly across the stomach, where it interfered with the operation of both arms.

The door opened unexpectedly. Both Monk and Ham whirled. The pig, Habeas Corpus, squealed and scooted under a low bench.

The individual who had entered the room was both huge and unprepossessing of feature. His skin was brown, scarred, his lips thick, and he walked with a pronounced limp. He carried two swords across his middle instead of one, the hilts projecting on either side where they could be grasped conveniently.

"Sabah el-kheyr!" he roared.

"No savvy," Monk growled. "And who the heck are you to come busting in here? How'd you like to have a taste of your own ears?"

"That is no way to speak to a Tananese who merely greeted you with the top of the morning," the newcomer said dryly.

Monk swallowed twice, then exploded, "Doc!"

"Think the disguise will do?" Doc asked.

Monk grinned. "What's first on the program?"

"I am going out and roam through the streets," Doc advised. "Renny is going to serve as personal bodyguard to the Khan Nadir Shar for the time being. You two will go everywhere with Joan Lyndell, when she is not in her private quarters."

Monk snorted, "Am I going to find that job hard to take!"

Ham suggested hopefully, "Maybe Monk had better guard Oscar Gibson."

"My pal," Monk growled. "I oughta shake you out of the bundle of cloth you're wearing for a suit."

Doc Savage, his personality completely submerged in the Tananese disguise which he had donned, passed out through the door. His stride even matched the shuffling gait of the lower class of Tananese, a gait which had come of years of climbing mountains and of following slow-moving yaks.

Monk and Ham, their unusual garments—garment, rather —adjusted to the demands of propriety, if not to their own satisfaction, shuffled off and found Joan Lyndell. They were, at present, in her home.

The young woman occupied an exquisitely carved, throne-like chair on a raised dais which stood in the center of an enormous room, the walls of which were hung with tapestries.

She was holding a sort of court, a steady stream of Tananese passing before her, each sinking to his knees and touching his head to the floor, then speaking rapidly, or answering questions which the young woman put to them in the native tongue of Tanan.

Not all of the men spoke Tananese, however. Two or three individuals, instead of touching their heads to the floor, merely stuck out their tongues as far as they could. This, Monk and Ham knew, was a form of Tibetan greeting, and they recognized that these men spoke Tibetan.

Joan Lyndell answered them smoothly in their own language, and Monk and Ham, who comprehended that language, realized that these were representatives of the girl's trading company, reporting conditions to their chief.

Behind Joan Lyndell sat two stenographers, taking down the important details of what was said.

There finally came a man who made a report that, from the girl's expression, was very disturbing.

She turned to Monk and Ham.

"One of my trusted officers, a man occupying a position to correspond with that of a vice president in an American company, has been absent from Tanan during the time I myself was gone," she advised meaningly. "He returned only to-day."

Ham had scorned the blunt Tananese sword which had been furnished with his native garb. He wore his own sword cane belted across the front of his stomach, instead of the other weapon.

"You think he might be one of the Mystic Mullah's men who was in New York?" he asked.

"Those men were killers," said the girl. "This man is not that type. He is Shallalah El Auwal, a man whose ancestors have been chieftains as far back as Tanan history goes. If he went to New York, it is reasonably certain that he is the Mystic Mullah."

"What are we going to do about it?" Monk asked grimly.

"We will go and speak with this Shallalah El Auwal," Joan Lyndell said grimly. "Where is Doc Savage?"

"Out looking around," Monk advised.

"Then we will go alone," said the young woman.

The "alone" proved to be somewhat exaggerated. Fully two hundred heavily armed guards accompanied them, surrounding them, and a party went on ahead, beating drums, shouting and jostling the ordinary citizenry into side streets.

But through the pomp and noise, Monk and Ham could see things. Tanan was a city of terror. Children are usually present in the streets of Oriental cities, hordes of ragged urchins being the rule. There were none abroad here. Nor were there any women out. All of the men to be seen were heavily armed, and more than one slunk away in a manner which showed a guilty conscience.

There was something else which smashed home the grisly nature of the situation. At frequent intervals along the streets there were piles of stones, these being surrounded with prayer wheels which spun noisily with every vagrant breeze.

Atop each mound lay a body, and in each case, the dead man had a broken neck. Some of the corpses had been on their strange biers a number of days, judging from their bloated aspect.

"They started putting the bodies in the streets while the Khan Nadir Shar was gone," Joan Lyndell said hoarsely. "They say that the Mystic Mullah decreed that this was to be done, on pain that the relatives of the dead man would also die. The true motive, of course, was to add to the spell of horror which the Mystic Mullah has been building up.

"The Khan has ordered it stopped, and the bodies removed. They do not seem to be removing them, however. And that makes me afraid that an uprising is close at hand, when the Mystic Mullah will try to seize the government."

"People in Tanan continued to die while the Mystic Mullah was in New York?" Monk asked wonderingly.

"Yes." The girl nodded. "And they say the Mullah also appeared here each day, before different persons."

"But he couldn't if he was in——" Monk shook his head, let that sentence go unfinished, and said, "It beats me!"

That Shallalah El Auwal was a personage of importance was evident from the magnificence of his dwelling and the number of his retainers. The palatial residence covered some acres, being situated inside a courtyard which was circled by numerous small houses.

"It is the custom in Tanan, as in many Oriental countries, for all the poor relatives of a rich man to come and live with him," Joan Lyndell explained. "The poor relations occupy the small dwellings."

Shallalah El Auwal himself, it developed, lived in the glittering edifice set in the central portion of the court. Joan Lyndell directed her cavalcade toward this.

"If the guy is the Mystic Mullah, we'd better be careful," Ham suggested.

"We will be careful," the girl agreed.

She gave orders, and her men spread out, encircling the central dwelling. Monk and Ham eyed the girl's personal guards distrustfully, however, for they could detect a certain slouchiness in their manner, a surly undercurrent which indicated that they were not to be depended upon too greatly.

"Bet about half of them mugs have gone over to the Mystic Mullah," Monk breathed.

"It looks like this whole thing is a powder keg," Ham said, forgetting himself so much as to agree with Monk.

Unexpectedly, from within the house of Shallalah El Auwal a great babble of yelling arose. There were screams, wails. Gongs clanged.

"I figured there'd be trouble," Monk announced grimly. "They're gettin' ready to put up a scrap."

"Wait!" Joan Lyndell said sharply. "Something has happened!"

She ran forward, stopped just before the door of the house, and called out sharply and repeatedly until she got an answer. Then she came back to Monk and Ham.

"We misjudged the Shallalah El Auwal," she said slowly.

"Whatcha mean?" Monk demanded.

"He is dead," said Joan Lyndell.

The uproar in the house of unfortunate Shallalah El Auwal was getting louder, coming nearer the door. Soon a procession appeared, several men coming first, carrying a ponderous platform affair upon which rested the body of a man.

"It is Shallalah El Auwal," Joan Lyndell affirmed, then turned so as to look away from the corpse.

A man came up to the young woman and spoke rapidly. Joan heard him through, then translated for the benefit of Monk and Ham.

"Shallalah El Auwal was threatened by the Mystic Mullah, who demanded all of his wealth," she explained. "Shallalah El Auwal hid himself away, letting it be said that he was absent from Tanan. To-day, one of the mountain chiefs sent him a present of a pretty dancing girl, and her charms caused him to show himself. That was his death."

"His neck is not broken," Monk decided after eying the dead man again. "What killed him?"

"A human spider," Joan Lyndell replied.

"Huh?" Monk was puzzled.

"Listen," said the girl. "They are bringing the spider now."

A group of screaming women appeared at the door, and after some struggling about, got themselves outside. They numbered nearly a dozen.

"The wives and dancing girls of Shallalah El Auwal," Joan Lyndell offered.

The excited women were doing a strange thing. Each held the end of a long rope. These radiated from a common center like spokes from a wheel. At the central focus point of the ropes, an extremely pretty young Tananese girl was tied. Her clothing was torn, and she was bruised; cuts in her smooth brown skin dripped scarlet.

One of the wives holding the ropes dug a cobble out of the courtyard and hurled it at the girl prisoner. It struck and bounced off with a sickening thud. Another of the wives drew a knife, screamed madly and dashed forward.

"Blazes!" Monk gulped. "That ain't no way to act!"

He started forward, roaring, and brushed through the fringe of wives until he reached the woman with the knife. There was a brief flurry, during which Monk, trying to be gentle, all but got stabbed; but the homely chemist secured the knife. Then he sprang toward the girl to whom the ropes were tied, evidently with the idea of freeing her.

Joan Lyndell, racing to Monk's side, yanked him to a stop.

"Don't be a fool!" she snapped.

Monk scowled at her. "Listen, lady, this may be an old Tananese custom, but it gets under my skin. I'm going to turn this girl loose!"

"Don't you realize what she is?" Joan Lyndell demanded.

Monk snapped, "I know she's a danged pretty little kid who——"

"Is a human spider," finished Joan Lyndell.

Monk blinked, wet his lips, opened and shut his huge hands, then looked from the Tananese girl to the remarkably beautiful young American girl before him.

"Human spider," he mumbled.

"Look at her finger nails," Joan advised.

Monk did so.

"They could stand manicuring," he admitted. "But I don't see nothing else wrong."

"See the yellowish deposit under the nails?"

Monk looked again. "Sure."

"That is a poison which is almost instantly fatal," said

Joan Lyndell. "That girl has but to scratch you, and you will die. That is what killed Shallalah El Auwal. She is the dancing girl who was sent to him as a present."

Monk studied the pretty Tananese. "Darned if I believe it."

Joan Lyndell spoke to the wives, and got a conglomeration of excited replies.

"The girl has confessed," Joan translated. "She was sent by a chief in the mountains, at the order of the Mystic Mullah. It seems that the green soul slaves of the Mystic Mullah were unable to kill Shallalah El Auwal, and the more prosaic method of the human spider had to be used."

"Prosaic!" Monk exploded. "You mean this sort of thing is common in Tanan?"

"Not common, exactly," the young woman replied. "But it has happened before. In Afghanistan, it is even more often practiced."

"Whew!" Monk gulped. "What will happen to this girl—this human spider?"

"She will stand trial," said Joan Lyndell.

Monk sighed jerkily.

Ham shook an admonishing finger at the apish chemist and said, "Let this be a lesson to you."

"Whatcha mean, shyster?" Monk growled.

"Before you start shining up to one of these Tananese girls, give her a close manicure," Ham told him.

Chapter 15

SINISTER CONFERENCE

The enormous bodyguard which Joan Lyndell had brought with her on the visit to the house of unfortunate Shallalah El Auwal, had seemed unnecessarily large at first; but now, as the return trip was started, it began to look as if the force was not overly adequate. They had scarcely left the walled compound which enclosed the house they had visited when it became apparent that word of their presence there had spread, and with ominous results.

There was a throng outside, an ominous multitude which gorged the streets. There were only men in the crowd. These stared sullenly at the array of guards. Some muttered under their breath; others yelled out maledictions.

"They say that the Mystic Mullah has spread the word that the mother of every man in Tanan will have her life taken by the green soul slaves unless I am slain, the Khan Nadir Shar deposed from power, and Doc Savage and his men slain," advised Joan Lyndell.

Ham fingered his sword cane uneasily, eying the ominous street crowds. He fished under his voluminous garment and made sure that no folds of cloth were in the way, should he want to draw his machine pistol suddenly.

Joan Lyndell ordered their guard forward. The latter formed themselves in to a thin spearhead and forced a way through the streets. The throng gave way, but many yells jarred out, and occasionally a stone or a short spear came through the air.

"I can see why the Mystic Mullah wanted to do his fightin' here instead of in New York," Monk said grimly.

Monk's pet pig, Habeas, emitted a series of uneasy grunts, as if his porcine mind comprehended their danger.

"You'd better throw that hog away and get ready to run," Ham advised. "Our escort seems to be getting cold feet."

This was true. The spearhead of soldiers was shrinking, literally wearing itself away against the crowd. Watching, Monk and Ham saw one guard after another seize his chance and duck away into the throng.

Joan Lyndell called out angrily, but it had no effect. The guards continued to desert. There was a worried expression on the young woman's face now, and she carried her automatic pistol in plain view.

"These guards were trained by my father," she said grimly. "I had hoped they would be faithful."

Monk put Habeas Corpus down so as to have both hands clear.

"They don't intend for us to get back to your house," he told the young woman.

She nodded. "We will head for the castle of the Khan Nadir Shar."

She rapped a sharp order. The guards who remained hesitated, then swung sharply to the left and dived into a narrow street. The throng of Tananese had not expected this, and angry shouts went up.

"Bet they had an ambush arranged ahead," Monk offered.

"Imshi bil 'agal!" Joan Lyndell called sharply to their escort. "Go more swiftly!"

The escort swung into a trot. This side street was narrow, not pleasing to eye or nostril, and was populated largely by yaks, donkeys and dogs. There was a chill wind blowing down from the mountains which enwalled Tanan, and steely clouds in the distance suggested snow.

Along the street, prayer strips fluttered in the wind and prayer wheels spun like toy windmills. Underfoot, grimy snow was packed hard by the pad of innumerable yaks, the shaggy Himalayan ponies known as *tats,* and human feet shod in clumsy felt boots.

The way began to lift, surmounting a hill. This prominence was surmounted by an extremely large building, portions of which they began to glimpse through the spaces between houses. This had been pointed out earlier to Doc and his men as the official *yamen,* or palace of the Khan.

"Look!" Monk grunted suddenly, and pointed out a certain figure mingling with the populace who were slowly closing in on them again. The figure was that of a giant brown man of unprepossessing features.

"Doc!" Monk breathed. "He's keeping an eye on things."

They lost sight of Doc Savage shortly, and did not again sight him before they came out in a wide open space which surrounded the walls of the *yamen.* They raced madly across this area.

A few arrows discharged from short, stout bows hissed about them, or struck in the quilted armor of the guards without doing harm. Ham dodged wildly and let a spear go past. Then they were crowding over an ancient drawbridge and through an embrasured wall.

The Khan Nadir Shar himself met them, and when they were over the draw, he sprang out and, his hook-nosed face livid with rage, bellowed at the throng. Some of these yelled back. Then they slunk away.

"Six months ago, no man in Tanan would have dared raise his voice against me," the Khan said grimly. "It is very bad. I fear for our safety."

Lifting his voice, the Khan called out loudly, and a moment later a stocky, utterly ferocious-looking man came striding up. He wore, instead of the conventional robes of the Tananese, a long *pushtin,* a fleece-lined leather coat of the type popular with the Russians.

His head was entirely bald and exposed to the rigors of the chill air. Strapped to his middle were two revolvers; a pair of cartridge bandoleers crisscrossed his chest, and a very modern automatic rifle was slung over one shoulder. Two short daggers and a stubby sword completed the picture of a walking arsenal.

"This is Mihafi, commander in chief of my army," said the Khan. "Of his loyalty, I am certain."

Monk and Ham studied Mihafi, and were not greatly impressed. This, they recalled, was the individual whom Oscar Gibson claimed had tortured him into admitting falsely that he was one of the Mystic Mullah's agents.

Mihafi, for his part, gave Monk and Ham a somewhat too elaborate bow and an oily greeting in Tananese, which they could not understand.

"He affects me like carbolic acid," Monk told Ham when they were alone.

Mihafi went about the business of posting the castle guard with hardboiled efficiency. Whenever he detected a sign of sullenness among the guards, he immediately detached the guilty individual and ordered him booted through an embrasure into the moat, from which the unlucky one might climb if too many of his bones were not broken. The moat was frozen solid.

Projecting from the walls of the castle were rows of steel spikes. These sloped downward, and were intended to prevent any one scaling the walls. Men were put to touching up the needle points of these spikes and greasing them with yak tallow, so that they could not be used as hand holds.

Fires were lighted in the court, under huge kettles which

were filled with lead to be melted, that it might be poured down on the heads of any so reckless as to try to scale the walls. Too, ancient flame-throwers of the Chinese type were prepared—hollow tubes filled with a concoction of sulphur and other substances which would spew flame and molten liquid upon the attackers.

"Looks like a party," Monk offered dryly.

Mihafi, having overseen these preparations, confronted Monk and Ham, bowed with what he thought was military snap, and spoke in several different dialects and languages. When he tried *bod-skad*, the language of Tibet, he made himself understood.

"It is a wise turtle which grows a thick shell, and a smart tiger which sharpens its claws," he imparted. "We are now ready for these dogs who have given their souls to the Mystic Mullah."

"You are doing well, O Man Without Hair On His Head," Monk admitted.

Mihafi looked as if he did not care for the form of address.

"This mighty bronze man who came with you—where is he now?" he asked.

"Search me," said Monk, then did his best to translate that into *bod-skad*.

Mihafi looked disappointed. "The fox that is wise retires to his den when the dogs begin barking," he said.

"Doc can take care of himself," Monk grunted.

Mihafi's ugly features took on a more ferocious aspect.

"This one who is named Oscar Gibson, where can he be found?" he questioned.

Monk tried his hand at the Oriental method of making replies.

"He who tries to know all things only makes himself dizzy," he stated.

Mihafi walked off looking puzzled, as if not sure whether he had been given a hint to stop his questioning.

Mihafi entered the palace of the Khan, and his evil face took on an expression of cupidity as he surveyed the richness of the furnishings. He paused to finger a rug which had come from Turkestan, and over which an entire family of skilled rug makers had probably labored for years. He lifted a small gold image, judged its weight, and held it to the light that he might examine the jewels which encrusted it.

He went on past the little cubicles which housed the slaves of the Khan's household. Slavery still existed in Tanan, open bartering being carried on with human beings as the merchandise. Raiding the ferocious hill tribes for young captives who would bring a good price on the market, was a popular source of income to the violent young warriors of Tanan who could devise no other means of getting money. Such forays had laid the foundation for many a Tananese fortune.

Deeper into the castle, Mihafi penetrated. The passages were dark, and he produced a candle of yak tallow and lighted it by the ancient method of flint and steel. Going on, he came to a massive door crossed by heavy iron bars. He blew out the candle.

The door rasped faintly in the intense darkness as Mihafi opened it and passed through. After that, an intense silence and an infinite blackness swallowed him.

The quiet persisted for perhaps five minutes. Then the door gritted open again and some one came in. Shortly afterward, there was another arrival, and another, until fully a dozen persons had let themselves into the shadowy chamber.

The silence was not interrupted for a time. Then a volley of sharp gasps sounded.

Hanging in the air, apparently in the center of the gloomy subterranean room, the hideous green face of the Mystic Mullah had appeared. It revolved slowly, as if it could penetrate the darkness with its lurid eyes and view those who were present. The first words added to that impression.

"You are all here, my faithful," the macabre voice of the Mystic Mullah intoned. "That is well, for we must lay plans."

"The people of Tanan have been aroused as you directed," said one of those present. "They are as a flock of sheep who hear the howling of the wolves. At a word, they will fall upon those that rule and tear them to pieces."

"It is well," murmured the Mystic Mullah. "But it is also an unwise farmer who destroys his entire crop because there are a few weeds. He would better pull the weeds."

"Truly, your wisdom is great," said the other. "But what do you mean?"

"This bronze man, Doc Savage, must be slain," said the Mystic Mullah. "He is a devil with the strength of a tiger and the cunning of one who has lived long in perilous ways."

"We are here to be told how to kill this bronze man?" the other questioned.

"No," the Mystic Mullah stated monotonously. "That has been arranged. You have been brought here to be told that the white woman, Joan Lyndell, is not to be harmed or molested."

Utter silence indicated that this proclamation was totally unexpected.

"This lowly one craves the light of knowledge," muttered a voice. "Why is she not to be touched?"

"Because it is she who will slay the bronze man," announced the Mystic Mullah. "Go, you who are faithful, and see that you harm the white woman not."

There was stirring in the darkness, and those who had gathered there began filing away. They did not strike lights, and none saw the face of any of his fellows.

Chapter 16

SURPRISES

Monk, pulling off his enormous felt boots, complained, "What dog cases! What dog cases!"

"Don't you ever get tired of grousing?" Ham demanded sourly.

Monk glared at the lawyer and advised, "Your pants are coming off, or maybe it's your shirt."

Ham scowled, and hastily adjusted the single enveloping cloth which was serving him as coat, shirt and trousers. Usually, he wore his clothing with debonair stylishness, but he had failed to master the technique of making the national garment of Tanan serve its purpose.

Renny came in, a giant form in coarse, dark cloth, with the glint of a short sword across his middle, and a bandage around his head.

"Doc hasn't turned up yet," he rumbled. "I'm kinda worried."

"He's hunting Johnny and Long Tom," Ham said.

Renny nodded. "If we had the slightest idea of where to look for them, I'd say that we do the same thing. But, holy cow! There's no clue worth following."

Monk looked up sharply. "Then there has been some trace of Johnny and Long Tom?"

"Only rumors," Renny advised. "The Khan Nadir Shar sent out some of his soldiers, and they found the planes which the Mystic Mullah used in the flight from New York. They found no one, naturally. But they did locate a peasant who had seen the ships land, and that fellow said there were two prisoners, both white men, who were carried away, blindfolded."

"Wasn't there the slightest trace of where they went?" Monk asked plaintively.

Renny shook his head. "None."

Monk began pulling his felt boots back on.

"Danged if I feel like sleeping," he muttered. "Let's prowl around the *yamen* until Doc comes back, or something turns up." He stood up. "Or until Oscar Gibson puts in an appear-

116

ance." He added as an afterthought. "I wonder what became of that lad?"

They went out on a balcony, a sort of outthrust of masonry surrounded by a parapet which was perforated with loopholes. It was night. The view was impressive, and not pleasantly so.

Fires had been lighted around the *yamen* at some distance, and Tananese stood in the warmth of these, mumbling among themselves, or staring at the high walls of the castle. More than one was openly sharpening a knife or a sword, and at intervals, an arrow would be discharged at the walls.

Over to the right, a group was rigging up a crude catapult, employing the springy trunk of a tree. They loaded this with a rock the size of a small keg; then fully fifty men seized a rope and sprung the tree back. One of them cut the rope with a slash of a short sword, and the stone was launched and sailed over the *yamen* walls, to crash through the roof and set guards to cursing.

"If a few knights were around in armor, the picture would be complete," Ham said dryly.

Overhead, the sky was a cold blue, with the steely snow clouds now black humps over the distant mountains and the stars marvelously white flecks, like luminous snow suspended close above.

The view lost interest for Monk and the other two after a while. Anyway, it was cold outside, and the chill wind had an unpleasant way of whistling up inside their blanketlike garments. They went inside.

The felt boots made little noise on the stone floors, and this probably accounted for what happened next.

"Ps-s-t!" warned Ham. "Look!"

Ahead of them, barely distinguishable in the pale light, a figure crept. There was such stealth in the marauder's movements that suspicion was instantly aroused.

"Whoever it is is making for the part of the *yamen* where Joan Lyndell is staying," Ham breathed.

Then he glided forward. Monk and Renny followed, using care not to drag the felt boot soles, keeping their hands over hilt and tip of their swords in order that the steel might not rasp against the stone walls.

The figure ahead passed close to a brazier in which burned a blue fire of *teyzak,* and the uncanny glow illuminated his features.

"It's Mihafi!" Monk muttered.

Mihafi, patently unaware that he was being shadowed,

crept on and reached a narrow door. This he opened, but he did not pass through. Instead, a file of men came out, half a dozen swarthy fellows whose deportment was as sneaky as Mihafi's. They whispered together, then moved on.

"Making for Joan's room," Renny growled faintly.

Mihafi reached the door of the chambers occupied by Joan Lyndell. Then he and his men shed all caution. That took Doc's three aides by surprise. They had expected Mihafi to continue his stealth.

Mihafi dashed a key into the door lock, turned it and boosted the panel open. Inside the room, Joan Lyndell shrieked.

Monk emitted an angry howl and charged. Monk liked to yell when he was fighting. Renny and Ham flanked him, grimly silent, Ham with his sword cane out.

Mihafi's brown men whirled, clawing at their short swords. An instant later, the corridor was filled with lunging men and the rasp and clank of colliding swords.

Felt-covered feet slapped in the passage behind Doc's men. They threw glances backward. What they saw was far from pleasurable. Mihafi had evidently not taken all of his men with him, but had left some behind, and these were staging a flank attack.

Enclosed on both sides, the three men backed hastily against a wall. Monk threw his short sword, and it spiked into a brown shoulder. Then the homely chemist hauled out a machine pistol and it moaned.

The brown men wavered. Some began to weaken as the mercy bullets took effect. Then these victims were seized by their fellows and used as living shields behind which a renewed charge was staged.

Joan Lyndell was still shrieking. There was more of anger than fear in her voice. She appeared, being dragged by Mihafi and three other men.

Monk leaped up in an effort to get a shot at Mihafi, but the fellow was canny and ducked down, whisking the prisoner around an angle in the gloomy stone corridor.

The brown men lunged in furiously upon Monk and the other two. They were concentrating on preventing Mihafi from being followed. Some one threw a knife, and the blade opened Ham's hip slightly. Renny lost the bandage which he was wearing over the ear that a Tananese bullet had damaged in New York.

All three had their machine pistols out now. They used them carefully, keeping them in their left hands, warding off an occasional violent rush with the short swords in their right.

Eventually, they broke through the fringe of assailants and raced in the direction Mihafi had taken with his captive. Around the first corner they plunged. Their quarry was nowhere in sight.

Nor did they find Joan Lyndell.

It was fully fifteen minutes later, and they were still searching, when the Khan Nadir Shar joined them. He looked worried and he was heavily armed, attended by a group of personal guards, huge fellows. Some one had told him of the uproar, he declared, adding that his own quarters on the other side of *yamen* were virtually soundproof and he had not heard the tumult.

Doc's men recited rapidly what had happened, and the Khan heard them through with an expression of growing horror on his hawklike face.

"This is very bad," he groaned. "The white woman, Joan Lyndell, was one of my staunchest supporters and most trusted advisors. She had an influence in Tanan equal, if not exceeding, my own."

They searched further, but finding no trace of Joan Lyndell or her captors, returned in the direction of the young woman's quarters.

"Holy cow!" Renny exploded when they came within sight of the door and that portion of the corridor in which the fight had taken place.

The corridor was empty of Mihafi's followers who had dropped in the fray. There had been bloodstains on the corridor floor. These were now gone.

"But, blast it, them guys couldn't have walked off!" Monk growled. "And some of 'em got cut up pretty bad. What's become of the blood?"

The door of Joan Lyndell's chambers opened, and to their utter astonishment, the young woman herself appeared. She was entrancing in a robe of silk.

"What has happened?" she asked.

Monk let his jaw down on his chest as he stared at her.

"How'd you get loose?" he demanded.

"Get loose?" Joan Lyndell shook her head slowly. "I don't understand."

"Huh!" Monk strode swiftly to her, shoved past and looked over the room beyond, lifting tapestries, peering into recesses, until he was sure no one was there forcing the girl to speak in the manner she did.

"What is the meaning of this?" the young woman demanded sharply.

"After Mihafi carried you off, how'd you get loose?" Monk questioned.

"Mihafi?" Joan Lyndell shook her head. "I never saw him. He certainly did not carry me anywhere. I have been asleep. Your noise here in the corridor awakened me."

Doc's three men exchanged bewildered looks, then shifted glances to the corridor itself, which was so mysteriously empty of bodies and bloodstains. There was nothing to show that the fight and the kidnaping of the girl was anything more than an evil trick of their imaginations.

Joan Lyndell stood perfectly still, relaxed, and there was certainly no fear upon her face. In fact, she was smiling slightly, as if she believed the whole affair were some kind of a joke.

"Are you sure you are not suffering from hallucinations?" she asked.

Monk absently felt of his machine pistol, then drew it out and, examining it, saw that the ammo drum was well over half empty. It had been full at nightfall.

"I dunno," he muttered. "It depends on what it takes to make a hallucination."

After the girl had returned to her chambers, Monk, Ham and Renny stood for a time and conversed with the Khan Nadir Shar.

"It is very mysterious," said the Khan.

"Mysterious, hell!" Renny thumped. "It's downright impossible! It couldn't have happened!"

"Many fantastic things are caused to happen by this Mystic Mullah," advised the Khan. "Perhaps there was no fight and no capture of Joan Lyndell."

Ham touched his hip where the knife blade had slit the cloth.

"If it was a dream, it was entirely too lifelike," he said, grimly.

The Khan shook his head slowly and muttered, "Sometimes I wonder if this monster, the Mystic Mullah, is really not what he claims to be—one who lived and died before time began, and whose soul has existed through the ages, absorbing the knowledge of all infinity."

"Nuts!" Monk said. "That whole idea is cuckoo. It *couldn't* happen."

"Nor does it seem that you could indulge in a fight when there was seemingly no fight," murmured the Khan.

Shortly afterward, the Khan retired in the direction of his

rooms, accompanied by his guard of huge dark men, and Monk, Ham and Renny moved in the direction of their own quarters. They wanted to discuss the affair privately.

Doc Savage was there, much to their pleased surprise. The bronze man was somewhat disheveled, as if he had moved about a great deal.

"Find Long Tom and Johnny?" Monk asked eagerly.

Doc shook a slow negative. "The best I could do was to pick up rumors of two white devil ghosts who are being held by the faithful of the Mystic Mullah," he said. "That will be Long Tom and Johnny. But I could get no definite line on them."

"Tough!" Monk muttered.

Doc said, "You fellows look a little strange! What is wrong?"

So they told him what had happened, dwelling particularly on details of the fight outside the girl's room, as if they wanted to impress upon the bronze man that the fray could not have been a dream.

"How do you explain it, Doc?" Monk finished.

"Go to sleep," the bronze man suggested. "Forget about it. Get some rest, and we'll tackle this thing in the morning."

Renny boomed, "But Long Tom and Johnny——"

"The Mystic Mullah will have to make some move before we can get a line on them," Doc said. "Turn in, you fellows."

They turned in.

Ham, who was somewhat of a nervous man, was a light sleeper. It must have been well past midnight when he awakened, for the air had turned bitterly cold, and the noise of the Tananese gathered around the *yamen* had died away.

Knowing something must have awakened him, Ham gripped his sword cane, with which he habitually slept when in danger, and lifted quietly on an elbow. He suspected that the noise had been made by Habeas Corpus. The pig had an aggravating habit of dragging Ham's shoes away, to chew on during the night.

But Habeas had not made the noise. There was a stirring in the darkness across the room. A vague shape took form before Ham's staring eyes. It changed position, moving out into a ray of moonlight.

Ham all but shouted aloud, so great was his shock. He stared more intently, wondering if he could be mistaken. But the features of the marauder were outlined with perfect distinctness.

It was Joan Lyndell.

The young woman walked slowly, making little noise. She was headed directly across the room—and Ham, shifting his stare, saw Doc Savage seated on a pile of rugs, his back to the wall. The bronze man's head was tilted forward and he appeared to be asleep. The girl was making furtively toward him.

Amazement held Ham motionless and silent for the moment. Then he shifted cautiously, moving back the felt coverings of his couch. For greater warmth, he had gone to bed fully attired. But his feet were bare and the utter coldness of the floor caused him to shiver. Or perhaps it was the attitude of the girl.

She was half crouching now, and her hands were out before her, fingers distended in resemblance of claws. She was staring at Doc steadily.

She came into another shaft of moonlight, and her shapely form stood out in brilliant silver. She leaned forward and seemed to set herself.

"Doc!" Ham screeched. "Look out!"

Had the bronze man been asleep, it was doubtful if he would have escaped. But Ham knew, even as he yelled, that Doc was only feigning slumber, for the bronze man moved with incredible speed, not changing the position of his body, but shooting up his hands and grasping the wrists of the girl.

The next instant, Ham had reached them and was helping hold Joan Lyndell. The girl struggled violently for a moment, then became quiescent in their grip. She did not cry out. Her exquisite face showed no emotion whatever.

Ham shuddered violently and choked out, "Look at her finger nails! That dark yellow stuff under them!"

Monk and Renny came stumbling in, weapons in hand, blinking sleep away.

"What's goin' on here?" Monk barked.

"Joan Lyndell," Ham said thickly, "is a human spider!"

The shock of the announcement held Monk and Renny speechless for a time. Indeed, they did not show full belief until they came over and inspected the young woman's finger nails and saw the deposit of poison.

"This explains what happened this afternoon," Monk mumbled. "The girl lied about the fight and about Mihafi seizing her."

"But why did Mihafi grab her?" Renny thumped.

Instead of answering, Doc Savage went to their baggage and got out a nail file, small orange sticks and a swab of cotton. He brought these to the place where Ham held the girl.

"Hold her hands open," he directed. "Don't let her move. If some of that poison gets into her bloodstream, it will probably kill her."

Joan Lyndell had been quieter when the bronze man was not before her; but now, as he grasped her wrist, she struggled wildly, as if in the grip of an insane frenzy, and it took much of the bronze man's strength to hold her.

He went to work on her finger nails, carefully cleaning them of the poison deposit, afterward swabbing under each nail with cotton.

The poison he placed in a glass phial, perhaps for later analyzing and study, should he ever return to his New York laboratory.

The girl had not spoken a single word.

"What are we going to do with her?" Monk growled.

Doc glanced sharply at the homely chemist.

"Don't you see what has happened to her?" he asked.

Monk frowned. "She's acting queer. She don't say anything. But maybe she——"

"She is hypnotized," Doc told him.

"Huh?" Monk made a round hole with his mouth.

"You know something of hypnosis," Doc told them. "A person once put under a spell can be made to forget all events which they are told to forget. In addition, they may be told to do a certain thing at a later time, and when the designated time comes, they automatically go into another hypnotic spell and perform the suggested act."

"Holy cow!" Renny breathed. "Mihafi got the girl and somebody hypnotized her and made her forget what had happened. Then she was told to put poison under her finger nails and try to kill you. She did it. She doesn't know what is happening."

Monk snapped his fingers violently.

"Listen!" he rapped, "can she be made to tell who hypnotized her?"

Doc told him, "I was going to see about that."

The bronze man then went to work while the others watched. That Doc was an expert on the vagaries of the human mind, that he had studied hypnotic suggestion from the masters, the holy men of India, they knew. They had seen him work his power before.

Doc worked for a long time, talking gently, making movements with his hands, and the girl finally began to talk. Her voice was far away and strange, as if she were not speaking, but her vocal cords were being actuated by remote control.

"Where did Mihafi take you?" Doc asked her.

She spoke, but the words were unintelligible, and the bronze man repeated his question.

"I was blindfolded," the girl said thinly. "When they uncovered my eyes, we were in a dark room. Then the Mystic Mullah came."

"Who was he?" Doc asked.

"He was a face, a green face that hung in the darkness without body," was the reply.

"That don't help us much," Monk grunted.

"Quiet," Doc told him. Then to Joan Lyndell: "Do you remember anything about the room?"

"There was a sound of thunder that did not cease, nor grow louder or weaker," the girl stated in her strange voice. "And when doors opened somewhere in the darkness and men came down steps, they brought with them the odor of sandalwood."

"Anything else?" Doc asked. "You are sure you do not know who the Mystic Mullah is?"

"Nothing else," said the girl. "And I do not know the identity of the Mystic Mullah."

"Blast it!" Monk grumbled. "That ain't gonna do much good."

Doc Savage now escorted Joan Lyndell out into the corridor, and there, holding her attention with a sword blade dangled in front of her eyes, brought her out of the hypnotic trance with sharp commands.

The young woman, awakening, stared about in amazement, not understanding what had happened, not remembering anything.

"Why—why——" she stuttered, and swallowed. "What am I doing here?"

"You must have been sleep walking," Doc told her. "We heard you."

"Goodness!" she gasped. "I never did that before!"

Then she fled, coloring prettily.

Chapter 17

CLUE OF THUNDER AND SANDALWOOD

It was possibly fifteen minutes later that Oscar Gibson appeared. He looked rather neat in the coarse cloak which was the common Tananese garment.

"Where you been?" Monk growled.

"Out picking daisies," said Gibson.

Monk glared and rasped, "Listen, you little snort, I still don't go in for your idea of being funny, and one of these days I'm going to give myself the satisfaction of rolling you out flat!"

Gibson smiled, "My, what a temper!" and ambled off.

Monk stood up, yawned and said, "I think I'll take another look around before I try to get some sleep."

"You'll need some one to watch you, you ape," Ham advised, and followed Monk out into the corridor.

"Let's follow this guy Gibson," Monk whispered. "I don't like the cut of his bib or the way his lip flaps. I don't trust him, even though Doc seems to."

"He saved Doc's life back in New York when the green things appeared in the yacht club," Ham reminded.

"Sure," Monk said. "And I'll remember that when his time comes. But I'm still in favor of trailing him."

"You and me, too," said Ham. "But if we get in a jam, remember—it was your fool idea. I'm just going along to keep you from gumming up things."

"I'd take it as a favor if you'd go off and die," Monk grumbled.

Trailing Oscar Gibson proved to be comparatively easy, for the thin-waisted man merely roamed along in the direction of his private quarters. He entered and closed the door loudly.

"If I recall rightly, there's a balcony outside his window that he can leave by," Monk whispered. "Let's check on that."

They eased around, found that the door into the adjacent chamber was open, and crept through the arched opening. It was intensely dark. They were scarcely halfway across the room when both men stopped. They could hear some one

125

working at the window, some one who was on the balcony.

Monk and Ham both retreated hastily and took up a position where they could watch the room without being seen. They saw now why Gibson was leaving his chamber by the balcony. The region about the door of his own room was lighted by a flickering wick blazing in a can of yak tallow. As it was, Gibson was very hard to see as he left the room, and he was almost upon Monk and Ham before they saw him. They back-tracked hastily.

Gibson was more difficult to trail now. He worked over toward the central part of the enormous castle and eventually entered a chamber in which the odor of sandalwood was almost overpoweringly strong. In the center of the room stood a raised platform of richly matched stone, and on this stood an elaborate throne, from which led a strip of costly carpet.

"The royal throne room," Ham breathed.

"Shut up!" Monk whispered back. "Do you want that guy to hear us?"

Oscar Gibson crossed the throne room and passed through a door and down another short passage.

This part of the castle seemed to have been equipped in more modern fashion. For one thing, the rooms were warm, whereas the far side of the *yamen* had been bitterly cold. Monk, looking about for the source of heat, got a surprise.

"Lookit!" he whispered. "An electric heater! Blast it, I didn't know the place was fixed up with electricity. Wonder why we didn't get quarters in the modern part of the castle?"

Ham said, "Look at Gibson! Meeting some one!"

Oscar Gibson had not exactly met some one as yet, but he had halted and was knocking on a door. It opened. There was a short scuffle in which Gibson thrust a foot into the crack of the door, then spoke in a low voice. Toward the end, he used English; and Monk and Ham heard him distinctly.

"You fool!" Gibson said to whoever was inside. "The Mystic Mullah sent me over here. Doc Savage is not as dumb as we figured. He's suspicious. You are to hide me out."

The man inside said something that was inaudible.

"Well, wait until you get word from the Mystic Mullah if you don't believe it!" Gibson snapped.

After that, the man to whom Gibson was talking stepped out where he could be seen plainly. He was a broad figure in a leather *pushtin,* with numerous bandoleers of cartridges slung about his chest. He had an utterly ferocious face.

"Mihafi!" Monk grunted. "What do you know about that? The lug is still in the castle!"

Gibson and Mihafi strode along the corridor. There was now nothing particularly furtive about their manner, and this caused Ham to surmise grimly, "I'll bet half the castle guard are in with the Mystic Mullah."

Mihafi opened a door, stood aside to let Gibson through, then followed himself. He left the door open.

Monk and Ham put on a little speed, considering themselves hot on the trail that would lead to the Mystic Mullah. Their enthusiasm possibly made them somewhat careless. They listened at the door, heard distant footsteps of two men, then stepped boldly through.

It is almost impossible for a fully clothed man to move in the darkness without making some slight sounds. Folds of clothing are almost sure to rub together. So when men leaped upon Monk and Ham, they had a split-second warning.

Monk howled at the top of his voice. He always howled when he fought. Simultaneous with the howl, he ducked and lunged forward. His arching fist hit hard bones thinly padded with flesh.

Ham was cautious enough to have his sword cane already unsheathed. He lashed it out like a whip. A man screamed terribly and the blade bedded itself deeply enough that it had to be yanked free.

A terrific blow smashed Monk's back. It was caused by a man, jumping feet-first. The homely chemist went down. Men piled upon him, jumping, stamping.

Monk's methods in a free-for-all were remarkable. He grabbed a leg, and taking a lesson from the alligator, spun around and around. He held the leg tightly. The victim tried to turn. He failed, screeched; his leg bones gave with a distinct snap.

A gun went off, its flame a red spurt. Masonry, lead-loosened, clicked on the floor. Some one fell on Monk's face, stifling his yells. Two more men got his feet.

About the same time, a flying wedge hit Ham. He slashed one down with his sword cane. Weight of numbers bore him back. He tripped over a fallen form. The floor was very hard when he hit it.

Furious blows rapped. Men grunted. Monk moaned under the chest that was mashed against his face. After that, there was only the breathing of men who had worked violently.

"Excellent work!" said Oscar Gibson's voice. "But it was a bit noisy."

The shot had carried through the *yamen*, and excited cries

were now heard. Feet pounded as a man came running. Evidently he was not one of the Mystic Mullah's henchmen, because he stopped the instant a tallow candle was lighted and the glow fell upon the scene.

"*Wallah!*" he bawled, then whirled and fled.

The Mystic Mullah's men cursed, and four shots were fired by the one who had the gun. All four missed. The gunman swore and ran into the light of the candle, reloading.

The gunman was Oscar Gibson.

The *yamen* guard, who had happened upon the scene, got away, thanks to the running ability of a jack rabbit. He must have learned his lesson, because he did not cry out an alarm. He reached the old, cold part of the castle, still traveling at headlong speed, and there he crashed into Doc Savage.

"What is it?" the bronze man demanded in Tananese.

The frightened guard told his story by gasps.

Renny galloped up in time to get a gesture from Doc. They left the scared guard and raced for the scene of the combat. There was a good deal of shouting now, and men ran about, gripping their short swords, carrying candles or small copper pans of tallow in which a twist of felt burned.

Doc Savage reached the spot where Monk and Ham had fallen. He found the rock fragments which the bullet had chipped from the wall. That alone told him he was on the spot—that, and when he turned a flashlight on the floor, traces of wet crimson which had been wiped up too hastily.

Of the victims and their captors, there was no sign. Doc moved about, questioning guards, but could find no one who knew anything and would admit it.

Renny rumbled angrily. They were completely checkmated. He continued to rumble as they made their way back through the big throne room where the air was full of sandalwood.

Electric lights were burning now. They had been switched on by the guards. Doc Savage halted suddenly and collared one of the *yamen* sentries.

"Where does the power for these lights come from?" he asked, speaking Tananese.

"From a round, fat, black monster who rumbles and whose veins pump an invisible fire that burns the unwary," explained the guard.

"It comes from a generator," Doc translated for Renny's benefit.

The big-fisted engineer was not interested in the electric plant.

"Wonder if Joan Lyndell is safe?" he rumbled. "Maybe we'd better check up on her."

Doc nodded, and they sought out the young woman's quarters in the frigid portion of the *yamen*. There was no answer to their knock on her door, and the panel, which should have been locked, gave under their shove.

"Probably she's out seeing what the shooting was about," Renny said.

Then his long, gloomy face slackened, his huge hands strayed in small aimless gestures, and he tried to make words that seemed to refuse to form.

Joan Lyndell's automatic pistol lay on the floor. Near it was a torn half of blanket, and close to that a blanket strip which had been rent from the other portion. It was such a strip as might have been left over when several were torn to bind the young woman.

"The Khan!" Renny roared.

Doc Savage was already racing in the direction of Khan Nadir Shar's apartments. Long before they reached the door, they saw a guard sprawled in the hall, his head split open.

Inside the Khan's chambers there was some confusion, enough to show there had been a fight, and a little blood was red and wet on the floor. The Khan was not there.

"Doc!" Renny growled. "There's just you and me now!"

They were still standing there when some of the *yamen* guards arrived and discovered that the Khan was missing. Instead of wailing out the Asiatic method of expressing sorrow, they seemed happy over the event. Several showed white teeth in wide grins.

They did not grin so widely when Renny showed them the business end of a machine pistol. They knew what the weapon was, and permitted themselves to be herded into the Khan's apartments, where Doc used a hypodermic needle on each; they all went to sleep shortly. Doc hauled the body of the murdered guard inside, then closed the door of the Khan's quarters and made it tight.

"This whole thing will blow wide open the minute it is learned the Khan has disappeared," he surmised.

"Yeah," Renny agreed. "He and the girl were all that kept the Mystic Mullah from taking over things. I think it was the girl more than the Khan."

"Listen," Doc suggested.

A window was undoubtedly open somewhere near, and they could hear an ugly babble of sound—shouts, cries, the hammering of drums. They sought a balcony which projected above the frozen moat far below, and looked out into the brilliant moonlight of the late night.

The multitude about the *yamen* had aroused itself, had picked up its arms and was preparing to do something. The crowd was closer to the walls than earlier in the night. Occasionally a gun went off, or an arrow, launched hard, slithered along the stone walls or split its shaft.

The cries of the throng were for the most part unintelligible because of their intermingling, but now and then one yell did stand out.

"The Khan is dead, his soul now one of the green slaves of the Mystic Mullah!" was one of the cries.

"The female white devil ghost, Joan Lyndell, is no more!" was another yell.

The throng milled about, and big two-man muzzle-loaders went off, vomiting volumes of smoke; archers sent more arrows.

Watching closely, Doc and Monk discerned men going through the crowd, howling and screaming and shoving persons about, and by their very vehemence, getting the mob into some resemblance of a fighting array. These organizers—agitators, too, judging from their howling—were undoubtedly chosen of the Mystic Mullah.

From the peak turret of the *yamen*, a powerful electric searchlight came on, a startling and modern thing in this mad scene of almost medieval confusion. Its beam stirred about like a rigid white finger, and superstitious Tananese fled from it wildly at first, as if fearing its white magic; then, finding themselves caught in it and unharmed, they jumped up and down, beating their chests and squawling, grown both brave and angry.

But the searchlight beam seemed to turn a light on Doc Savage's agile mind.

"Come on!" he rapped.

The bronze man ran back into the endless stone passages of the vast *yamen*, descended steps that were centuries old, and sought about until he found a fat castle servitor.

"Electric generator!" Doc rapped. "Where is it?"

The flunky batted scared eyes and shook his head.

"The fat iron monster who roars and pumps invisible fire through his veins," Doc said. "Where does he lurk, this monster?"

The lackey got that, waved his arms and erupted a gibberish volley.

"Show me!" Doc clipped.

The plump vassal was none too willing, but a look at the

giant bronze man showed him what course was wise, and he led the way at a waddling gallop.

They went through the throne room where sandalwood was cloying in their nostrils, and shortly beyond, were guided into a steep stairs which led down. They could hear, once heavy wooden doors were opened, the rumble of a steam turbine and electric generator, both of which seemed to need new bearings.

"Good!" Doc said, and dismissed the domestic, much to the fellow's relief.

The bronze man went back to the throne room. He made a circle of the place, eyes busy. Renny watched him, coughing a little because the smell of sandalwood was so stifling. The stuff came from a brass affair near the throne and Renny finally moved over and dropped a rug upon the source of the perfume.

The odor was even stronger near the throne, and Renny, looking up, saw that the stuff escaped through a round ventilating aperture above. This was open and he could see cold-looking stars through it.

Doc came to his side.

"So you've got the idea," he said.

"Huh?" Renny was bewildered. "What idea?"

"Remember what Joan Lyndell said about the place where she was hypnotized?" Doc asked.

Renny scratched his head.

"You mean about the steady thunder and the odor of—holy cow!" Renny's mouth fell open, snapped shut. "Whenever the door of the place opened, she could smell sandalwood! She must have been right in here!"

"No," Doc said. "The sound of the generators cannot be heard here. That must have been the steady thunder which she heard."

"Sure!" Renny roared. "Sure! Why didn't I think of that?"

Doc waved an arm. "Get back."

Wonderingly, Renny retreated from the vicinity of the great throne.

"The odor of sandalwood is strongest around the throne," Doc said. "There must be a secret door leading into an underground room such as the one which holds the generator. And it is probably close to that perfume box you just covered up."

Doc dipped into a pocket and brought out two grenades not greatly larger than pigeon eggs. Renny saw them, and promptly whirled and ran to get farther away. He knew what those grenades would do.

Doc hurled the first one. The flash hurt their eyes; the roar hurt their ears even more. The elaborate floor split. The rich rugs gathered up in the great wind of the blast and piled against the walls; one sailed up as if attached to invisible strings and skittered about in the air.

Running forward, Doc saw that the grenade had opened no secret entrance. He retreated and threw another. Huge blocks of the roof came down. The floor split wider, and Doc, racing ahead again, looked down into one of the cracks and saw that it had opened in the roof of a passage.

He dropped down into the black maw. Renny followed him. Behind them, parts of the throne room ceiling were still falling down, making tremendous noises.

Chapter 18

THE GREEN FACE

Doc Savage raced his flashlight beam down the passage. Clouds of dust boiled in the air. In that fog, a jewel seemed to flash, traveling with eye-defying speed. Renny felt himself seized and jerked aside by Doc Savage even before he could realize the glinting thing was a thrown knife. It clanged on the stone behind them.

Renny yelled and ran forward, pushing his own flashlight beam out before him. He saw brown men, two of them. One had a knife. He threw it, and the blade was easily evaded. The pair appeared to have no other weapons, for they spun and raced away.

"Them's two of the guys who helped grab the girl before she was hypnotized!" Renny roared.

They charged down the narrow tunnel, pursuing the brown men. A murmur, faint at first, became louder, and since they already knew what it was, it was easily identified as the rumble of the motor generator set.

The brown men were screeching for help. They dived into a chamber which was very dark, the floor slimy with earth moisture.

Doc and Renny, overhauling them, were well over a third across the cavernous place when a hollow voice caused them to wrench to a stop. They swung in the direction of the eerie tones.

A face had appeared, the hideous green visage of the Mystic Mullah, swinging in mid-air as it always did. The lips writhed, seemed to snarl.

"It was convenient of you to come here," the voice advised.

Renny jerked his flashlight around, intending to turn it upon the satanic, ghostly visage, but something the light disclosed caused him to stop the beam.

Grisly green serpentine things were crawling through the air toward them. Hideous and fantastic, the horrors seemed alive, yet unreal. The flash beam, passing through them, hit the wall, and there were only vague shadows to show that the green objects were real.

Then there came a cataclysmic roar and a flash that seemed to turn Renny's brain to fire. He knew instantly, as he was tumbled backward as by a giant hand, that Doc Savage had thrown another of the grenades, and before he recovered himself the big bronze man had a hand upon his shoulder, urging, "Run!"

They ran for the door, but Doc Savage paused and switched his flash back. The wall where the green face of the Mullah had appeared was considerably torn up, and a slab of stone had fallen in, uncovering an opening of some size.

The Mystic Mullah himself was not in sight.

But out of the hole in the wall, like monsters from a cave, came the green monstrosities. They were true monsters, now, for some were a yard thick, great, squirming nebulous dragons, without shape or method of movement.

Renny, halting and glaring at the green things, bellowed, "Why, dang it! I see what them things are now!"

He started forward.

"Stay back!" Doc Savage's voice had a smashing power that wrenched Renny to a stop.

"I'll take a chance!" Renny howled. "That Mystic Mullah is in there somewhere!"

"If that green stuff touches you, it'll kill you!" Doc said grimly. "He was using two kinds. One only burned the skin and produced senselessness. The other was mixed with the venom of the neotropical rattlesnake."

"Neotropical——"

"Something like that," Doc rapped. "Venom of the neotropical rattler centralizes its effects in the nervous system around the nape of the neck and causes a form of nerve destruction which makes it appear that the victim has a broken neck. This poison probably had additional ingredients which heightened its effects, causing a muscular constriction which actually snapped the vertebræ in most cases."

Renny shifted in an endeavor to peer into the hole in the wall, at the same time avoiding the green horrors.

"But, holy cow, the way these things move!" he growled.

"Always launched so that a current of air will carry the green mist toward the victims," Doc said, and himself moved to glance into the wall opening. "Probably the stuff is squirted from some kind of a pump gun. That would give the snake-like effect."

Renny roared, "But they're bigger now!"

"Which means the pump was ruptured by the grenade, possibly," Doc said.

They drove their lights into the aperture. The green, smoke-like cloud of poison vapor filled all of the passage beyond the hole, but through its transparent body they could see a sprawled form, a figure enfolded in rich clothing.

It was impossible, however, to make out the features. But Renny boomed a guess.

"The Mystic Mullah!" he thumped. "The guy got his own medicine!"

The streamers of green poison were filling out into the room. Moreover, yells indicated an approaching attack. So Doc and Renny spun and raced on in pursuit of the two brown men who had fled.

Near the door, Renny tangled in an affair of wires, and fell back. He got up, growling, and turned his light on the contrivance.

"Blazes!" he gulped. "Here's how he stuck that green face around and made it disappear!"

The thing Renny had fallen over must have been blown across the room by the grenade blast. It was such a device as fake spiritualists and magicians sometimes use to make luminous heads appear in thin air—a telescoping tube of some length, to the end of which was fixed a thin-walled rubber balloon face which could be inflated by blowing through the tube; then, by suction, drawn back into the tube, and the telescoping affair collapsed. Manipulation of thin threads caused the appearance of lip motion.

Renny threw it aside, scowling as he recalled his own horror when he had first seen the thing in action.

They went on. Some one shot at them with one of the Tananese-made guns, but did not hit them, and Renny poured a deafening volley from his machine pistol. An instant later, they were in hand-to-hand conflict with four or five Tananese.

The latter were under an enormous handicap, in that they possessed, for light, only pans of tallow in which felt wicks burned. The flashlights in the hands of Doc and Renny blinded the others, and they did not last long.

Renny pumped mercy bullets into the fourth man, and Doc sank the fifth senseless with a tremendous fist smash.

They ran ahead, came unexpectedly into a chamber which was illuminated a pale pink by a heating brazier.

On the floor reposed tightly bound figures, mouths stuffed with wads of cloth. The apish Monk was nearest, and Ham was behind him, trying to free the homely chemist; beyond them were Joan Lyndell, Johnny, Long Tom and Oscar Gibson.

There were none of the Mystic Mullah's men left in the room.

Doc and Renny went to work untying the prisoners, and there was much pointless shouting, largely to let off steam.

Monk, rearing up on his feet, glared at Oscar Gibson and howled, "You got us into this, you smart-cracker!"

Gibson said wearily, "I was desperate. I tried to trick Mihafi into taking me to the Mystic Mullah. How was I to know you were following me?"

"That reminds me!" Ham snapped. "Where's Mihafi?"

They did not learn the answer to that until some five minutes later, when Renny ventured back to the room where the green poison vapor had appeared, and finding the vapor had strained out through ventilating apertures, stepped in and looked closely and long at the face of the Mystic Mullah.

He came back looking stunned.

"Mihafi is in there with him, down the passage a bit," Renny mumbled. "Say, did you know that the Mystic Mullah was——"

"He showed himself to us," Joan Lyndell put in jerkily. "And he made it clear why he had become the Mystic Mullah. He felt his power slipping. He was afraid I would eventually become the real power in Tanan. So he began operating as the Mystic Mullah to fight me—and to satisfy his desire for a great empire."

"Holy cow!" Renny muttered, "I didn't dream the Mystic Mullah was the Khan Nadir Shar."

They did not think they were remotely near a complete escape from their difficulties, for the populace of Tanan was laying siege to the *yamen*; but, as it developed, the situation was not serious.

Joan Lyndell, appearing on the *yamen* walls, managed to muster the loyal portion of her own guards. These, with the castle force who had remained faithful, fell upon the throng and there was violent fighting. The guiding genius of the Mystic Mullah, the Khan Nadir Shar, was sorely missed, and after a few hours, and somewhat before the noon hour, the thing was over.

Once it became bruited about that the Mystic Mullah had been the Khan, rage seized the Tananese, and they turned upon the Mullah's faithful. Those who had lost relatives to the so-called green soul slaves of the Mullah, were especially bitter, and lives were taken all through that day, the ensuing night, and, for that matter, throughout the months that followed.

Doc Savage and Joan Lyndell managed to take a certain amount of control during the confusion, and established a representative government of leading Tananese. This body strengthened itself, soon becoming stable, so that peace returned, menaced only by grudge killings as some wronged Tananese evened scores with one who had gone over to the Mystic Mullah. But Tanan was a savage, medieval land, and there had always been such feuds.

Doc Savage and his five aides left Tanan as soon as they perceived conditions had attained moderate stability. They traveled east, flying across the Gobi, and as Tanan was lost in its mountain cup, Monk declared himself.

"If I ever seen a stranger country than that, I'll let Ham make that traveling bag of Habeas Corpus's hide," he declared.

And Monk, little dreaming, recklessly offered to contribute Habeas's hide to the cause of good luggage, as their plane volleyed over the caravan trail eastward across the Gobi.

FREE CATALOG
of over 650 Bantam Books

- All The New Releases • Best-Selling Authors • Chilling Mysteries • Thundering Westerns • Startling Science-Fiction • Gripping Novels • Anthologies • Dramas • Reference Books • More.

BANTAM BOOKS
CURRENT

This fascinating catalog of Bantam Books contains a complete list of paper-bound editions of best-selling books originally